Pemberley's Christmas governess

A Pride and Prejudice Vagary

by Award-Winning Author

REGINA JEFFERS

REGINA JEFFERS

Chapter one

Mid-December 1818 - Gloucestershire

"I said to unhand me, sir," Elizabeth Bennet ordered, as she shoved young Mr. Newland's hands from her person. Ever since the man had returned home, he had dogged her every step. She had been serving as the governess for his two younger sisters for six months now, but this was the first time the lieutenant had been home since her arrival at his parents' home.

"I just be luckin' for a bit of fun," Mr. Newland slurred as he attempted to kiss her ear, but all she received was a wet lash of his tongue across her cheek. He reeked of alcohol.

Elizabeth wished she had been more careful when she left her room a few minutes earlier, but she had briefly forgotten how the lieutenant seemed always to be around where she least expected it. She had thought him below stairs with his friends, both of whom had been excessively respectful to her. She shoved hard against his chest sending him tumbling backward to land soundly upon his backside. "If it is fun you require," she hissed, "join your friends in the billiard room!" Elizabeth side-stepped the man as he reached for her.

Lieutenant Newland attempted to turn over so he might stand, but he was too inebriated to put his hands flat for balance and to rotate his hips. "I don't be requirin' that kind of fun," he grumbled.

Elizabeth edged closer to the steps. She hoped to escape before Lady Newland discovered her with a torn sleeve and the woman's rascal son doing a poor version of standing on his own. "You must find your 'fun' elsewhere, sir. I am not that type of woman."

She had been a governess for nearly five years—five years since her dearest "Papa" had died suddenly from a heart attack—five years since her mother, Kitty, and Lydia had moved in with Aunt Phillips in Meryton, and Jane and Mary had moved in with Uncle Gardiner. Elizabeth, too, had been sent to London with Jane and Mary, but it had been so crowded at her uncle's town house, she immediately took a position as the governess to Mr. and Mrs. Gregory Sample's daughters, Livia and Sylvia. She had remained with the Samples, who were a wealthy middle-class gentry family and friends of her Uncle Gardiner, for a little over two years before the Samples brought the girls out into society and married them off.

In Elizabeth's estimation, Livia, at age fifteen, was too young for marriage, but the girl appeared happy with her choice of a husband. Sylvia, at seventeen, had been more reluctant to wed, but the girl had followed her parents' wishes. Few women had the freedom to choose their husbands, even in the lower classes, and certainly not in the gentry.

Elizabeth had spent another two years with another wealthy, but untitled, family, preparing their daughter for an elite school for young women on the Continent. In mid-May, she had answered an advert with an agency to join the Newland household. Although she had often thought Lady Newland was too pretentious, Elizabeth had enjoyed the enthusiasm of her young charges: She had considered them to be very much of the nature of her sisters Mary and Lydia. Pamela wished desperately to please her parents, but to no avail, while Julia was as boisterous and as adventurous as had been Lydia.

Elizabeth desperately missed her family, but, essentially, she knew their current situation was her fault. Such was the reason she had sacrificed herself by going out on her own—removing the responsibility for her care from her family's hands—one less mouth to feed and to clothe.

Jarred from her musings by Lieutenant Newland's lunge for her legs, Elizabeth squealed and scampered down the steps before the man could catch her. However, the lieutenant's momentum sent him tumbling down the stairs with a yelp of surprise—heels over head— to land spread-eagle on the floor, except one of his legs had been turned at an odd angle. A loud moan of pain escaped to echo through the hall.

The sound of running feet filled the open hallway. Immediately, Elizabeth dropped to her knees to examine the lieutenant's leg. "Permit me a look at your leg, sir," she told the man as she swatted away his hands, still attempting to grope her. "Lay back!" she instructed.

Immediately one of the lieutenant's fellow officers was beside her. "Lay back, Lieutenant," he ordered in a strong voice of authority. "Permit the lady to examine your leg." The colonel looked to her, and Elizabeth mouthed, "Bad break."

After that, the colonel took charge. "Mr. Scott, send someone for a surgeon." The butler rushed away. "You two, find some sturdy blankets and a board—a door, perhaps, so we might move Lieutenant Newland to his room."

"Yes, sir," the footmen scrambled to do the colonel's bidding.

Before Elizabeth could extricate herself from the scene, she looked up to view Lady Newland's worried countenance. It was all Elizabeth could do not to groan aloud. There was no hope that her ladyship would take Elizabeth's side in the matter. "Nigel! Nigel, darling!" Lady Newland screeched as she knelt beside her son. "What has happened?" She shoved Elizabeth from the way.

Colonel Fitzwilliam explained, "I have sent for a surgeon and a means to move Newland to his room."

Lady Newland nodded her understanding as she caught her son's hand to offer comfort. Unfortunately, for Elizabeth, the lieutenant rolled his eyes up to meet hers. "I'm thorry, Miss Bennet."

Lady Newland cast a gimlet eye on Elizabeth. "Sorry for what, Miss Bennet?" she aked in accusing tones.

Even though she knew such would cost her the position she held in the household, Elizabeth refused to tell a lie. "For the lieutenant's attempt to take liberties where they were not welcomed, your ladyship."

Lady Newland stood to confront Elizabeth. "Evidently, you thought one day to take my place as viscountess."

The colonel stood also. "I believe you are mistaken, ma'am. Both Captain Stewart and I have warned the lieutenant that it is inappropriate for a gentleman to take favors with the hired help. Your son's 'infatuation' has been quite evident to all who chose not to turn a blind eye to his thoughts of privilege."

Lady Newland pulled herself up royally. "I shall not listen to anyone defame Nigel's character. I realize you are my son's commanding officer, but I am the mistress of this house, and I say who is and is not welcome under my roof. I would appreciate it if you removed yourself from my home by tomorrow."

Captain Stewart joined them then. "Your ladyship, surely you realize the colonel is the son of the Earl of Matlock," he cautioned.

For the briefest of seconds, Lady Newland's resolve faltered, but she looked again upon Elizabeth's torn sleeve and stiffened in outrage. "You may stay, Colonel, if you wish to condemn the real culprit in this matter."

The colonel's features hardened. "Although it provides me no pleasure to say so, for the British Army holds a standard for its officers, even those of a junior rank, but I have named the culprit, ma'am." He bowed stiffly. "I thank you for your prior hospitality. I, for one, will depart in the morning after I learn something of your son's prospects for recovery so I might properly report the surgeon's prognosis to my superiors. Captain Stewart may choose to stay or depart on his own." With that, he extended an arm to Elizabeth. "Permit me to escort you to your quarters, Miss Bennet."

Though in the eyes of Lady Newland, Elizabeth's doing so was likely another mark against her character, she gladly accepted the gentleman's arm, for she did not think her legs would support her without his assistance. She was without a position and had no place to go.

"Are you well, ma'am," the colonel whispered.

"There is no way Lady Newland will provide me a letter of character. The chances of my securing another position without a recommendation are next to impossible. I shall be fortunate if her ladyship agrees to pay me the wages due to me."

The colonel responded in tones of obvious disapproval. "I will speak to Lord Newland regarding your wages."

Elizabeth attempted to keep the tears from her eyes. Until now, no one had cared that she was alone in the world. "You are very kind, sir."

"Not kind enough," he corrected. "Otherwise, I would have kept a tighter rein on Lieutenant Newland's actions."

"You are the lieutenant's commanding officer in military situations. You cannot also expect to be his conscience within the halls of his home," she argued. "Even if you had squashed his desires on this journey, you could not guarantee the lieutenant would not return alone some time in the near future. The encounter was inevitable."

"Your calmness amazes me, Miss Bennet," he declared.

"I am far from calm, sir," she said when they paused before the door to her quarters. "My insides are of the nature of a duck's legs under water. On the surface the duck appears serene, but his legs are beating out a tattoo."

The colonel chuckled. "Tell me you have a place that will take you in, at least until you can claim another position."

Elizabeth wished she could provide the gentleman the reassurances he required, but, at present, she had no idea where to turn. "Perhaps my aunt and uncle in Cheapside—"

"Once you have considered your choices," he said softly, "I would consider it an honor to assist you to your destination, if you will permit it."

Oddly, Elizabeth did not consider the man or his offer a threat to her person, as she had felt from the beginning with all Lieutenant Newland offered. "I thank you kindly, but I am not your responsibility, Colonel."

"My mother would argue otherwise. If she discovered I had abandoned you, there would be the Devil to pay for my lack of compassion. Do not tell her ladyship this, Miss Bennet, but I would rather return to the Continent and face the French a second time than to incur my mother's wrath," he said with an easy smile.

Elizabeth, too, smiled largely. "Your secret is safe with me, sir. Now, go to the lieutenant. I am certain he is in great pain, and a voice of reason must prevail in his care."

* * *

7

Elizabeth had managed to hold back her tears until she closed the door behind her. "What am I to do now?" she whispered to the sparsely decorated room. "My denial of Mr. Collins's proposal proved my mother's worst fears true." Charlotte Lucas's acceptance of Mr. Collins's hand within hours of Elizabeth's refusal had prevented Elizabeth from changing her mind. "Not that I would have done so," she sighed as the tears flowed freely. "At the time, I foolishly believed my opinions to be absolutes. Yet—"

Even after all the years that had passed, the idea of Mr. Collins touching her intimately brought a shudder of revulsion to her person. "Yet," she whispered once more. "Yet, if I knew then what I know now—if I could have saved my family from living as poor relations of my mother's siblings, I would have found a means to tolerate the man, just as has Charlotte." She smiled weakly. "I could have developed a taste for brandy or laudanum, something to dull the possibility of being Mr. Collins's wife."

Elizabeth pushed off from the door to have a look at her appearance in the small mirror on the wall. The sight of how her dress had been ruined brought on more tears. She possessed only a half-dozen gowns, all of which had been repaired numerous times. The thought of Lieutenant Newland's hands upon her had her wishing to rip the gown from her shoulders, sending the row of buttons flying across the floor. Allowing her to rid herself of the degradation she had endured. Instead, she wiped away her tears with the heels of her hands. It would be necessary for her to make do with what she had available. "Mama would be surprised to learn how much my needlework has improved," she told her weariness.

Not once to turn from the storm, Elizabeth swallowed the sadness rushing forward in an effort to claim herself. "No time to wallow in self-pity, my girl," she warned her wavering resourcefulness. "You have decisions to make and little time in which to make them. As I have been relieved of my duties, her ladyship's maid may tend the children this evening. I owe Lady Newland no allegiance in this matter. Instead, I shall use the hours ahead to repair this gown, to pack my portmanteau, and to weigh my options for the future. I have a bit of savings that can see me through as long as I can find another position within a few weeks. Likely, it is best if I return to London. I have missed my sisters terribly. A few days with family, yet, I shan't tell Uncle Gardiner of my situation. I shall just say I was presented an unexpected holiday. A few days with Jane and Mary and then I will find a cheap place to stay while I wait for news of my next post."

* * *

She had had a simple meal in the kitchen while she waited for the colonel and Captain Stewart to finish their breakfast in the morning room. Colonel Fitzwilliam had slipped a note under her door explaining how the surgeon had declared Lieutenant Newland's leg broken in two places, but such would not likely cause the man any permanent damage. The breaks would heal properly if the lieutenant permitted them enough time. The colonel delivered the lieutenant's apologies and Lord Newland's promise of a full quarter's wages.

Elizabeth had no doubt Lady Newland would have turned her out last evening if not for the colonel's interference. The gentleman apologized twice for not being able to secure a letter of character for her. Evidently, Lord Newland would not go against his wife in that manner.

Although no one in the kitchen had looked at her or acknowledged her in any way, when she stood to leave, Elizabeth defiantly said, "I enjoyed my time at Newland Hall. I pray you are equally satisfied with your time in service under the family." Her words could be construed as sadness or boldness: She would leave the interpretation to the hearer. Bending to reclaim her travel bag and portmanteau, she exited the house through the kitchen door—head held high. "Unbeatable," she said to fortify her spirits. "You are unbeatable."

* * *

Thursday, 17 December 1818

"There you are, Miss Bennet," the colonel said as she rounded the corner of the house.

"I apologize, sir, if I kept you waiting. I thought your note said nine of the clock."

"It did, miss," he said with an easy smile that Elizabeth thought likely served him well at society functions. The colonel was

9

not the most handsome man she had ever met, one Mr. George Wickham claimed that particular title, but she found his engaging personality a sincere advantage for the gentleman. "Permit me to assist you with your bags."

"I thank you, sir. I shall regret losing your tender care when I board the mail coach," she said with as much enthusiasm as she could muster under the circumstances. Elizabeth thought, *"Oh, for the days of six Bennet ladies crowded into Papa's coach."*

The colonel saw her into Captain Stewart's carriage before continuing their conversation. "Then you are set upon returning to London?"

Elizabeth said, "I do not see that I have much choice. If I am to seek another position, then I must be in London where the placements are posted more regularly than in the shires. I may spend a few days with my uncle's family before beginning my search."

"Are you certain your uncle will accept you, Miss Bennet?" Captain Stewart asked. "The colonel and I have spoken at length on the matter, and I agree with him that a lady should not be expected to ride on top of a mail coach all the way to London."

"I am not a lady, sir," she argued as tears misted her eyes, when she considered all she had lost.

The colonel shook off her statement. "You were raised as a lady, Miss Bennet. Your speech and how you carry yourself announces your upbringing."

"That was a long time ago, colonel. My father has passed, and my family is scattered across several shires. I possess no right to turn my nose up at traveling on a public coach."

"Then you are settled upon your plan?" the captain asked a second time.

Elizabeth swallowed hard against the maudlin filling her chest and throat. "I am simply thankful for a ride into Stow-on-the-Wold," she confessed.

The captain continued to question her. "What if the colonel and I offered you an alternative?"

Elizabeth's eyebrow rose in a mix of skepticism and fright. "I do not understand, sir. Are you or are you not traveling into Stow-on-the-Wood?" She sat straighter in preparation for a confrontation.

The colonel spoke first. "You see, Miss Bennet, Captain Stewart and I had a long conversation last evening. As our plans for Christmastide at Newland Hall have been interrupted, Stewart and I agreed to join my mother and cousin in Derbyshire. My father is on the Continent as part of a delegation conducting business for trade agreements for the British government. Therefore, the countess has agreed to host the gathering at my cousin's estate."

Elizabeth said cautiously, "I am pleased you and the captain have an alternative to your plans. Yet, I do not understand how your choice to join your family affects me."

"Bear with me," the colonel said. "Stewart and I thought you might wish to join us there."

A deep frown claimed Elizabeth's features. "At your family gathering? I am a governess, sir, and, although I am presently in a tenuous situation, I am not in the habit of accepting charity beyond a ride into the village."

"I am not offering you a holiday, Miss Bennet," Colonel Fitzwilliam countered. "There will be a number of children in the household, and my cousin currently employs an older lady who tends to his infant daughter. Mrs. Anderson served as his sister's nanny, but several others are likely to be housed at Pemberley over the next fortnight. They will require some sort of care. I, therefore, thought you might assist Mrs. Anderson or make yourself useful in other ways in exchange for a place to stay while you search for new employment. Moreover, impressing my mother could allay any damage Lady Newland might do to your reputation as a caring and intelligent choice of governess. A letter of character from the Countess of Matlock would set you in an enviable situation for life, opening doors to the finest families."

Elizabeth asked softly, "Do you honestly believe Lady Matlock would promote my service to others?"

The colonel grinned largely. "Did I mention I am the countess's favorite child?"

Elizabeth asked teasingly, "Are you an only child, sir?" She worked a handkerchief through her fingers in nervous anticipation. Could this offer be an answer to her prayers?

"I possess an older brother who is the heir to the earldom, but I am the countess's heir to an estate, not as large a property as the Matlock estate, but large enough to support comfortably a family of my own. As the war is over, I have been considering whether it is time for me to sell out." He shrugged nonchalantly. "That is more information than you required. Anyway, what of Christmastide at Pemberley and a possible recommendation from the Countess of Matlock? If nothing else, I will plead with Darcy to assist you in locating your next position. My cousin is a very influential man. Stewart, here, can tell you how it is not uncommon for my Cousin Darcy to snap his fingers and the whole world shifts to meet his pleasure."

"What the colonel says is true, Miss Bennet. Although my father is a viscount, even Lord Artemis Stewart would not dare to cross the Darcys of Pemberley. Mr. Darcy is quite influential."

Elizabeth could barely control her breathing. "This all sounds so wonderful, and I am appreciative of your gesture, but I cannot arrive on your cousin's threshold in the company of two men I barely know. No decent family would employ such a woman—one who dares to accept the kindness of not only one gentleman, but two. Lady Newland's accusations would require little proof to society."

"Naturally," Captain Stewart said, "but what if we hired a girl to travel with you?"

"I could not ask you to expend such funds on my account." Elizabeth stated firmly. "What if I take a coach to Derbyshire and meet you at your cousin's estate?"

The colonel frowned, "Such would be excessively dangerous, Miss Bennet. I could not be indifferent regarding my placing you on a public coach while we ride in comfort."

Elizabeth did not want to lose this opportunity for a new position. "Perhaps we could discuss this in more detail while I wait for the public coach."

The colonel smiled that charming smile Elizabeth had observed often on the man's lips. "Capital, Miss Bennet, for I sent Darcy an express last evening to inform him that, in addition to Captain Stewart, I would be escorting a young lady to Pemberley. My cousin will be expecting you."

Chapter two

Friday, 18 December 1818

Darcy stifled the groan rushing to his lips. He had always despised the necessity of making social appearances—constantly feeling from step with those who populated London ballrooms and, in this case, a local soirée, but he had promised his Uncle Matlock to squire the countess to a variety of local entertainments in exchange for Lady Matlock's agreement to host Darcy's annual Christmastide house party, the first since the death of his wife, nearly two years prior.

He had finally succumbed to family pressure and had married his cousin, Anne de Bourgh. He had certainly not loved Anne, beyond familial love that is, but he had become exhausted of looking for a woman who could stir his soul and assist him with the demands of Pemberley, as well as being tired of being hounded by, literally, a horde of society mamas and girls straight from the schoolroom, many younger than his sister Georgiana.

He had been a few months past the age of thirty at the time of his marriage to Anne, who had begun to blossom under his tender care of her person, and, for a few short months, Darcy had thought himself content, if not necessarily happy in his marriage, and he had convinced himself to know "satisfaction" would be enough, even if such was not the type of love his parents had displayed.

When Anne had become heavy with child, Darcy thought himself blessed, at last. There would be the possibility of an heir for Pemberley and more children. Unfortunately, just like her namesake, his sweet Anne had died from a long and difficult birth, leaving him alone and caring for his daughter Cassandra. Sometimes he wondered if his wife had simply not been up to being a mother, and he should have left her to her spinsterhood. He blamed himself for Anne's untimely death as much as he blamed her for not fighting harder to remain with him. The idea did not please him, but it stayed with him, nevertheless. His cousin certainly would never have served as his partner in running the estate. Anne permitted him and his long-time housekeeper, Mrs. Reynolds, to continue on without interruption at Pemberley House. Mrs. Reynolds still planned all the meals and oversaw all the household duties that Anne should have shouldered.

As he entered, Darcy sucked in a deep breath to "gird his loins" for what was to come. In society's eyes, a rich widower, especially one with a healthy fortune, was as likely to be in want of a wife as was an unmarried man.

His aunt handed her cloak to a waiting footman. "Wipe the snarl of disgust from your lips, my boy," she whispered. "A bargain is a bargain."

Darcy sighed heavily. "Might I not leave you in Roland's care? After all, this evening is in honor of your eldest's betrothal to Miss Ashley."

"Which is why you must stay. With both Matlock's and Fitzwilliam's absence, I do not want the Ashleys to think our family objects to Roland aligning himself to the young lady."

Darcy edged her closer to him as they climbed the stairs to the hall set aside for the evening's entertainment. "I forgot to tell you, right before we departed the house, I had an express from the colonel. It appears he and Captain Stewart will join us at Pemberley earlier than we expected."

"That is delightful news," Lady Matlock declared, her face lighting up with a large smile. "But what occurred at Newland Hall? I did not expect my youngest son to join us until after the turn of the year."

"You know Edward's tendency to omit important details when writing to his family," Darcy said with a matching grin. "When I receive a message from him, I always pray his military communications are more thorough. He simply said he would require three rooms."

Lady Matlock paused on the stairs. "Three? I thought you said only Edward and the captain would be joining us. Are we also to host Lieutenant Newland? I do not much care for the lieutenant's family nor the man himself. Lady Newland is, in my opinion, quite crass."

"Not Lieutenant Newland," Darcy confirmed. "Edward said, under unsatisfactory conditions, which your son promised to explain upon his arrival, Newland had broken his leg."

"Then who is the third party?"

Darcy leaned close to say. "A young lady, one of whom Edward hopes you and I will approve."

The countess caught at her heart. "Fitzwilliam is bringing home a young lady for the family's approval?" She reached out for Darcy's arm for support. "Darcy, say you do not misrepresent my son's message for your own sport."

He reached in his inside pocket to retrieve the note. "Read the colonel's words for yourself, Aunt."

Lady Matlock snatched the paper from his fingers to unfold it. "It is as you say, Darcy." He watched as a large smile claimed her lips. "What sort of young lady?" she questioned as her eyes searched the note.

Darcy turned her to the side so others could pass. Softly, he said, "Obviously, your son does not make a full explanation, but, knowing my cousin, Edward has considered the woman's place in society. Although his time in the military has the colonel not seeing the same strict guidelines of society as Roland does, Edward would never bring home, say, a woman of the muslin brigade to be introduced to his mother. Fitzwilliam's extensive military career provides him the ability to judge a person's merits by speech and deed, rather than by pedigree. In my opinion, we should both be happy that his heart has been engaged by a respectable woman, even if she is from the middle class or from a merchant family. She could even be someone of the gentry, whose family has known hard times of late. God only knows, since the end of the war, a large majority of the landed gentry is struggling. We simply must meet the lady with an open mind."

Her ladyship nodded her agreement as she continued to read the message. "He does not even provide us the lady's name."

Darcy said, "I, for one, will happily accept any woman who has captured Edward's heart."

Lady Matlock refolded the note and handed it back to Darcy. "As shall I. And, if the lady is not fully suitable, I will assist her transition into the Matlock family. You know what a stickler your uncle can sometimes be. He and Lady Catherine were cut from the same cloth. I do not know how your mother could be so different from her siblings."

Darcy said, "Even my mother and father could be unbending in many ways." He lowered his voice with a warning, "If the lady is also of age, there will be little Matlock can do to prevent Edward's marriage, if that is the colonel's wish. We simply must be happy if he likewise is." He grinned largely at her. "Perhaps between Roland and Edward you will soon hear someone call you 'Grandmother.'"

She barked a laugh. "I am saving that line, only substituting 'grandfather,' if Matlock lodges an objection to either of my sons' choices. He has often bemoaned the lack of the next generation of Fitzwilliams."

* * *

Two days later, Darcy and the countess welcomed the first of the few guests Darcy thought appropriate to host at Pemberley after his hiatus last Christmastide to grieve appropriately for Anne's passing.

"Bingley!" he called as he descended the stairs to greet his long-time friend with a firm hand shake. "I am very pleased you decided to join us."

"It has been too long since we were in company," Bingley declared with a smile on his lips. "You were sadly missed during the Season."

Darcy said softly, "My attendance would not have been appropriate. It was too soon." He had not loved Anne, but, nonetheless, he had grieved her passing, for she had always been a "beloved" cousin. He turned to gesture to his aunt. "You recall Lady Matlock."

"Most assuredly," Bingley declared with a proper bow. "My felicitations, your ladyship. Darcy has previously shared the good tidings of your eldest son's betrothal to Miss Ashley. I had the

16

pleasure of briefly taking the lady's acquaintance at the beginning of the most recent Season."

Although Darcy knew his aunt was not best pleased to spend Christmas with those whose wealth came from trade, she smiled kindly on Bingley and made him welcome.

Darcy turned to view Mr. and Mrs. Hurst and Miss Bingley, along with Hurst's children stepping down from the Hurst's carriages. He groaned internally, for he should have known Bingley's extended family would take it upon themselves to claim another invitation to Pemberley. In truth, Darcy had enjoyed their self-imposed abandonment of Pemberley during his marriage to Anne. Even so, he placed a smile on his lips.

He motioned Mrs. Reynolds forward to say softly, "You will see to additional rooms away from the family quarters."

"Absolutely," his housekeeper said with a click of her tongue in disapproval. "I understand, sir." With a few whispered instructions and a flick of her hand, she sent a handful of maids and footmen to do her bidding.

"Mr. Hurst. Mrs. Hurst. Welcome to Pemberley," Darcy said through a tight smile. "Mrs. Reynolds will see to your quarters as quickly as things may be arranged. Naturally, the nursery and school room will be open for your children. Mrs. Anderson, who tends my Cassandra, will be available to assist your nurse in settling in."

"We did not bring the nurse," Louisa Hurst announced with a lift of her chin. "I assumed Pemberley would possess adequate staff to address the needs of our children."

Darcy bit back the retort rushing to his lips. It would be necessary for him to have another private talk with Bingley to inform his friend that Darcy would no longer tolerate the Hursts and Miss Bingley, who was busy ordering Darcy's staff about as if she were Pemberley's mistress. The trio took advantage of every invitation from Darcy to Bingley, acting as if the invite had been meant for them all. He would despise losing one of his closest friends, but Darcy had abided the intrusion of Bingley's family on his life one too many times. If necessary, he would provide the Hursts and Miss Bingley a direct cut in Town, essentially ending any connection they wished to claim to his family.

Mrs. Reynolds diplomatically said, "Along with Mrs. Anderson, I will have one of the maids look after the children."

Lady Matlock's nostrils flared, indicating her disapproval of the situation. The Countess of Matlock's reaction to the gall of Louisa Hurst to foist her children's care on another was exactly as Darcy imagined his mother would have responded.

"Darcy, darling," Miss Bingley purred from beside him. She rose up on her toes as if to kiss his cheek, but Darcy, instinctively, leaned away from her before saying, "Welcome, Miss Bingley. Mrs. Reynolds will see you to your quarters."

Darcy had thought, with his marriage to Anne, to be rid of Miss Bingley's forwardness. Unfortunately, with Anne's passing and his mourning period essentially at an end, it was evident Miss Caroline Bingley meant to reinsert herself into Darcy's life. A private talk with Bingley was definitely in order. Regrettably, for Darcy, Miss Bingley's most loyal suitor, a man with whom everyone thought she held an understanding, had recently made an offer of his hand to another lady. At four and twenty, Caroline Bingley was, most assuredly, on the shelf. The lady was desperate, meaning Darcy must be on his guard.

As Miss Bingley followed Darcy's housekeeper up the stairs, Lady Matlock groused, "I know you are excessively fond of Mr. Bingley, but, even you, Darcy, must realize the inferiority of Mr. Bingley's relations. Obviously, Mr. Hurst cannot claim grand connections, despite being a 'gentleman.' You must cut ties with these people, and, obviously, have Mr. Sheffield sleep in your room for the time being. That chit means to be the next Mrs. Darcy."

Although he agreed with her, Darcy said, "Let us view who Edward brings to Pemberley before we cast stones. Perhaps Miss Bingley would be a better choice for your youngest son than the woman who accompanies him. If no other attributes you might wish your future daughter-in-marriage to possess, Miss Bingley has a sizable dowry, if a man had a need of it."

"Let us pray the woman in Fitzwilliam's company possesses attributes outweighing any of those Miss Bingley flaunts before you."

* * *

It was early afternoon of the third day of their travel when Captain Stewart's carriage entered the gate leading to the great estate of Pemberley. While both gentlemen napped, Elizabeth said a silent prayer that she might impress any of the guests at Pemberley enough for someone to provide her a lead on another position. "At least, I shall be safe and warm and fed for the next fortnight, even if I am presented a servant's quarters," she murmured.

"Pardon, miss?" the girl the gentlemen had hired as her companion asked as she roused herself from her sleep.

"It is nothing, Hannah," she said with a smile. "I was simply enjoying the view."

Hannah turned to look out the small window. "It is grand, is it not, miss?" the girl asked as she leaned across Elizabeth for a better look.

Elizabeth nodded her agreement. As they drove along, she had watched for the first appearance of Pemberley Woods with some anticipation. Although she had experienced a bit of perturbation, having heard so much of the splendor of the estate from both the colonel and Captain Stewart, she had been duly impressed by the entrance. Consequently, when the coach made the turn upon the lane leading to the lodge, her spirits rose higher, likely as high as were Hannah's, for the girl had had her own stories of Pemberley House, for Hannah had grown to adulthood in a village but five miles removed from the estate. Elizabeth's thoughts, therefore, had been based deep in anticipation.

It had been pure happenstance that the girl, who now served as Elizabeth's abigail, had recognized Colonel Fitzwilliam and had begged him to permit her to ride on top of the captain's coach when the mail coach had had no room for another servant girl on board.

The colonel had quickly made a bargain, which would permit the girl to travel with them as Elizabeth's maid and stay at Pemberley long enough for Elizabeth to settle in before Hannah would set out for Lambton.

Elizabeth's mind returned to the passing scenery rather than her worries of being turned away. Surely, Colonel Fitzwilliam would not permit that to happen, even if the Countess of Matlock disapproved of her son's actions.

From what she could observe of the estate's entrance, the park was large and contained a great variety of vegetation. She would have enjoyed viewing it without the coating of frost on the ground. The thought of the cold had her instinctively looking to her thread-bare cloak, which she drew closer about her shoulder, suddenly feeling a chill crawl up her spine, whether from the cold or her nerves, she could not say. At length, the coach entered the tree line at one of its lowest points and drove for some time through the woods, which stretched over a wide extent.

Elizabeth saw and admired every remarkable spot and view. After a few minutes, the coach gradually ascended for half a mile to emerge at the top of a considerable eminence, where the wood ceased, and the eye was instantly caught by Pemberley House, situated on the opposite side of the valley, into which the road, with some abruptness, had wound. It was a large, handsome stone building standing well on high ground, and backed by a ridge of high woody hills, and, in front, a stream of some natural importance was swelled into greater, but without any artificial appearance. Its banks were neither formal nor falsely adorned. Elizabeth was delighted. It had been so long since she had enjoyed a long walk in nature, and, despite her chill from a few moments earlier, she prayed the unknown Mr. Darcy would have no objections to her doing so, as long as she spent several hours in service each day.

She had never seen a place for which nature had done more, even on a cold December day. The place's natural beauty had been so little counteracted by an awkward taste that she found it truly magnificent.

Eventually, they descended the hill and crossed the bridge, with the sound of the wheels on the wooden structure vibrating through the carriage, which woke the gentlemen, who quickly sat up and straightened the cut of their uniforms. Elizabeth found herself reaching for her hair to make certain her chignon had not slipped down beneath her bonnet.

As the coach rolled to a stop, the massive door to the house opened, and all of Elizabeth's apprehension of meeting the estate's owner returned.

* * *

"William, is it true?" Georgiana burst into his study without knocking. Darcy had purposely hidden away in his private sanctuary to avoid Miss Bingley's excessive attentions at tea earlier.

He smiled upon his sister. When he had finally agreed to marry Anne, he had hoped a marriage and a wife would provide Georgiana the confidence to face society after that debacle with George Wickham when she was but fifteen, but Anne had possessed her own insecurities, and, by the time Georgiana turned seventeen, the family had learned of Anne being with child, providing them all a legitimate excuse to avoid their social obligations. The delivery of his daughter had brought him and Anne such happiness, but that happiness had been short-lived. Anne had come down with childbed fever, lingering longer than any of the family thought possible, considering her frail condition. That was followed by a funeral. Then a year of full mourning. And before Darcy knew what was what, Georgiana was approaching a monumental birthday, one where she would turn one and twenty and claim her majority without ever having a London Season.

This gathering at Pemberley was to serve as a prelude to his sister's official Come Out. Such was the reason he had added several young ladies and gentlemen to the list of guests that would stay at Pemberley and to the events planned for the New Year's ball, thus, providing Georgiana the company of someone other than her elder brother to enjoy.

"Is what true, Georgie?" he said with a grin, as he came from behind the desk to claim her hand.

"Will Edward join us today instead of after the New Year? Aunt Matlock says it is so."

It had been nearly a year since Darcy had seen such delight marking his sister's features. "I had a note from the colonel on the day I escorted our aunt to the soirée. I am grieved that I forgot to mention it to you."

She grinned at him. "You are forgiven, Brother. I am too thrilled to have the colonel with us to chastise you. I have missed Edward's attentions, not that yours are lacking," she was quick to add.

"No offense taken." He squeezed her fingers. "I know you are quite fond of our cousin; yet, I must warn you that Edward may be too distracted to provide you his full attention."

His sister's features screwed up in confusion. "What could be more important to the colonel than family? That is all he has ever claimed to be his grandest wish: spending time with those he affects."

Darcy looked closely at Georgiana. Did his sister's interest in their cousin lie beyond the fact that Edward also served as one of her guardians? "I do not believe the colonel means to spend Christmastide alone. In fact, he will not arrive on our threshold without company."

Georgiana nodded her understanding. "The countess says Fitzwilliam travels with Captain Stewart."

Darcy corrected, "There is a third party traveling with them: A lady of whom Edward hopes both his mother and I will approve."

Georgiana looked as if someone had struck her. "A lady? Is she a friend of Captain Stewart? Surely our cousin does not mean to bring someone to Pemberley with whom he has developed a *tendre*."

"Neither the countess nor I know the colonel's intentions toward the woman," Darcy assured. "But, as our cousin has never shown more than a mild flirtation toward any female, both Lady Matlock and I think Edward seeks permission to present a particular lady his family's acquaintance, which makes this a monumental moment."

Georgiana's features displayed her confusion. "Who is this woman? Is she someone we know? What is her name?"

Darcy paused before answering to look toward the window. "I do not know the lady's name, but I suspect we are about to learn it. If I am not mistaken, that is Captain Stewart's carriage crossing over the bridge this very second. Come along." He tucked Georgiana's hand about his arm. "We will learn something of the colonel's mystery woman together."

Chapter three

As Darcy and Georgiana descended the steps, the main door swung open, and the image of his favorite cousin and most trusted confidant stepped down from the carriage to stretch for the briefest of seconds before greeting Mr. Nathan with a good-natured slap on the back. Spotting Darcy and Georgiana, the colonel crossed the short distance to the door and entered the foyer with a wide grin marking his lips. Darcy, instinctively, thought his cousin's actions odd, for, most assuredly, Edward should be tending to the lady serving as his traveling companion first.

However, before Darcy could lodge an objection or ask of the unknown lady, the colonel was striding toward him to catch Darcy up in a very masculine hug, slapping Darcy's back hard in a demonstration of affection. "Too long, Darcy!" his cousin declared. "Permit me to look at you." Edward leaned back and grinned again. "You age well, Darcy."

"Must be the Darcy blood," Darcy said with a shared smile to mark his tease. "The Fitzwilliam blood makes a man a rascal of the first tier."

The colonel laughed easily. "That it does, Cousin!" Edward turned immediately to scoop Georgiana into his arms. "You cannot be my sweet Georgiana," he declared with a wide smile of pleasure. "You are a fetching young woman. My Georgie is a thin wisp of a girl."

Georgiana giggled while slapping jovially at his chest with the back of her hand. "You must put me down, Cousin."

"I cannot," Edward asserted. "My heart is taken by the elegance of your countenance."

Darcy noted the look of pure happiness on his sister's face, but, before he could comment on it, from halfway up the stairs, the Countess of Matlock instructed, "Put Georgiana on her feet this second and present your mother a proper greeting."

Edward looked up with adoration marking his features. "Yes, ma'am." He kissed Georgiana's forehead and then climbed the stairs to present his mother a proper bow of respect.

"None of that," the countess chastised before wrapping her arms about him. Edward easily lifted her into the air, and, for the briefest of seconds, Darcy knew jealousy. He had been but twelve when he lost his mother, Lady Anne Darcy, and not a day had gone by that he did not wish to claim just such a moment for his own.

Driving regret from his features, Darcy turned to greet Captain Stewart. "We are pleased you have decided to join us, sir." He extended his hand in greeting. Outside, he caught a glimpse of a petite woman providing directions to what must be her maid and assisting Darcy's footmen to separate the gentlemen's trunks. A frown formed on his forehead. The lady should not be left to sort these things out.

"Welcome, Captain Stewart," Lady Matlock called as she descended the stairs on her son's arm.

The captain bowed properly and said, "Thank you and Darcy for accepting my presence along with the colonel."

"Always glad for more company," Darcy repeated, while searching the drive once again with his eyes for the woman, who, evidently, had disappeared.

Bingley and his youngest sister appeared to greet the new guests, and, so, Darcy slipped outside to ask Mr. Nathan what had transpired. "Where is the young lady, Nathan?"

"The lady insisted on following her abigail around the house to a 'less than obtrusive entrance.' She said she would speak to Mrs. Reynolds at the kitchen entrance."

"Ridiculous!" Darcy growled as he went after the woman. "Miss! Miss!" he called, using his long legs to overtake her. "Miss, there must be—"

The lady turned to look upon him, and Darcy forgot to breathe. An odd sizzle of recognition swept through him—an emotion he had never felt previously, but one which felt natural, nonetheless, despite it sending his normal complacency on high alert.

The lady was a good head shorter than he, but not quite as petite as he had first thought. Delicate, very feminine features and a fragile bone structure could not disguise the firmness of character he discovered in her expression. Moreover, the lady possessed the type of eyes in which a man could easily become lost. Intelligent eyes. They glistened from the cold, but when they looked at him, Darcy thought he could see a future that had long evaded his multiple attempts at consideration. They were green with a touch of woodsy brown. Whether he liked it or not, he suspected they would haunt his dreams tonight, but he took quick note that they were equally "haunted," providing the woman a hint of vulnerability—a look that made him want to reach out and tug her into his embrace and offer her his protection.

Holding his hands tightly in fists at his side to keep the tug of possession from claiming his good sense, he said stiffly, "There is some mistake, miss. You are to join us in the family part of the house. The colonel wrote specifically to ask that we welcome you into our home. Please permit me to escort you inside."

She stared at him with curious interest marking her features. A small smile tugged at the corners of her lips, and Darcy had the distinct feeling a smile on her lips might be his undoing. "I did not wish to interrupt the colonel's homecoming. He has spoken often of the wonderful times he has spent at Pemberley." She glanced around. "It is truly a magnificent estate, sir."

"I am pleased you find it so," Darcy said, as a smile also claimed his lips. "You should view it in the spring and summer when it is green and full of color."

She sighed deeply. "I would enjoy doing just that so very much. When I was—" The lady paused, giving her head a good shake. "My memories are not significant or of interest to you, sir."

Darcy was not best pleased with her response. He would have liked to hear more of her opinion of his estate and her memories, but, instead, he presented her a slight bow. "Permit your maid to take your bags—" He looked to the girl, who appeared familiar. "I have seen you before, have I not?"

The maid dipped an awkward curtsey. "Yes, sir. I be Mr. Crownley's daughter, Hannah, sir."

"Of course," he said. "I thought you away from home."

"I was, sir. In Gloucestershire."

Darcy nodded his acceptance. "I hope your mistress means to allow you to spend time with your family. Crownley will wish to see you for Christmas."

"I have already told Hannah she may spend as much time as she likes with her family," the lady explained.

"Good," Darcy stated. "Then permit Hannah and my men to secure your bags in your quarters, and come away with me." He offered the woman his arm. "The colonel's mother is eager to take your acquaintance."

She hesitated. "But I do not know your name, sir," she said with a pert lift of her chin and with what sounded of a tease in her tone.

He smiled easily, realizing it had been forever since he had felt this light-hearted. "There is no one about to introduce us. The colonel is in the house," he reminded her.

The lady glanced over her shoulder to the maid. "Hannah holds both of our acquaintances. Could not she perform the deed?"

Darcy could not look away from the lady's countenance. He said with another grin of satisfaction for the privilege of speaking to such an enchanting woman, "Miss Crownley, might you provide me the acquaintance of your mistress?"

The maid giggled, but she managed a proper curtsey. "Lard, I never thought—" The girl sobered immediately. "Mr. Darcy, may I give you the acquaintance of Miss Bennet? Miss Bennet, the master of Pemberley, Mr. Darcy."

"Charmed, Miss Bennet." He repeated with a bow. "If you have no objections, miss, I would see you inside the house. You must be quite chilled through standing outside for so long. Derbyshire winters are deceptively cold."

The lady curtseyed. "Charmed indeed, Mr. Darcy," she said softly, before placing her gloved hand upon his arm.

As he turned her steps toward the main entrance, in Darcy's mind, time slowed. Desire as he had never known found a place in his chest. Instead of the main door, he was half-tempted to lead her to a nearby folly and enjoy more of the lady's smiles. An insidious whisper pronounced her as his. Yet, when he reached the still open door, reality slapped him in the face.

"There you are, Miss Bennet," his cousin said as the lady left Darcy's arm to stand beside his cousin. Edward said, very precisely, "My lady, with your permission, I would give you the acquaintance of Miss Elizabeth Bennet. Miss Bennet, my mother, the Countess of Matlock."

Darcy looked on as the woman, who had just bewitched him with a simple smile, executed a perfect curtsey. "I am humbled, my lady, by your kind recognition." She glanced to the colonel and smiled largely. "Colonel Fitzwilliam has told me numerous tales of his family."

The countess arched an eyebrow that said she thought Edward's actions odd, as did Darcy, for his cousin had shared nothing of the lady with any of his dear family, but Miss Bennet had said something similar to him only moments earlier. Darcy's aunt smiled her "social" smile. "I believe I speak for all of the colonel's family in saying we will be most happy to learn more of you, Miss Bennet. For now, welcome to Pemberley."

From a place on the staircase, Hurst called out, "Now, now, boys. No way for children to act. Louisa, I say do, something!"

Mrs. Hurst caught one of the boys just as Mrs. Anderson came rushing upon the scene. The nurse presented the gathering in the foyer a quick curtsey. "I apologize, Mr. Darcy," she said, wringing her hands in obvious distress. "I be puttin' Miss Cassandra down for a nap, and the boys slipped out when Megs was called away to assist Cook. They followed their parents after Mr. and Mrs. Hurst left the nursery."

Mrs. Anderson wrung her hands as if she was fearful of Darcy's disfavor. He did not like the look on the woman, who had been very loyal to his family over the years.

He said, "No harm, Mrs. Anderson. I will ask Mrs. Reynolds to have Megs and another maid take turns in assisting you. I am grieved to have added to your duties. I will see you are readily compensated."

"I beg your pardon, Mr. Darcy. Might I be of assistance, sir? I would be happy to return the boys to the nursery and entertain them until the maid can return to her duties in the nursery." Miss Bennet's earnest expression said she spoke honestly. "Surely there are some items in the house that can be used to entertain the boys. Toy soldiers, perhaps, from when you and the colonel were younger. Most large households store such items away as the children age."

His cousin suggested, "The grey trunk. Hey, Darcy. We kept all our best cavalry in it."

Darcy nodded his understanding and looked to his butler.

"I believe it was placed in the attic some years back, sir. I can have someone bring it down immediately, Mr. Darcy."

"We should have done so before now," Mr. Darcy admitted, although, in reality, it should be the Hursts' responsibility to see that their children were entertained.

Miss Bennet immediately handed her cloak, bonnet, and gloves to Mr. Nathan and then climbed a few steps to claim the hand of first one of the Hurst boys and then the other. "Why do you not come with me? Mr. Darcy has promised us a treasure chest full of toys to explore together. Will that not be grand?"

The youngest of the two said, "Yes, ma'am."

The lady turned to Darcy. "With your permission, sir," she murmured.

Darcy attempted to keep the frown from his features, but he knew he failed. "I must object, Miss Bennet. It would be the worst of society to accept a young lady into my home as a guest and then expect her to perform the work of a governess. Neither I nor my household can impose upon your good nature in such a manner."

"I assure you, sir, I would not feel put upon in any such way. I prefer to make myself useful, and, as my position in society is one of governess, please permit me to assist you."

Without waiting for his permission, she turned the boys' steps toward the above storey and gracefully climbed the stairs to where Mrs. Anderson waited to show her the way. As her little party turned toward the nursery, he heard her say, "You must tell me your names. I am Miss Bennet."

"Governess?" the countess asked her son. "Did Miss Bennet say she was a governess?"

"Yes, she did," the colonel declared. A look of admiration marked his features. "Was it not wonderful how she quite readily took the matter in hand? I am very proud of how quickly Miss Bennet proved herself useful to Darcy."

"But—" the countess thought to lodge her objection, likely the same objection rushing to Darcy's lips.

Edward claimed his mother's hand and brought the back of it to his lips. "I will explain later, Countess. For now, I want to freshen my clothes, and, then, I wish to hear all there is to learn of both Roland and father. How is the esteemed Miss Ashley? Is a wedding date set?" He turned to the rest of Darcy's guests. "I will look forward to hearing something from each of you at supper." He looked to Darcy. "My customary quarters, I assume."

"Yes, and the captain is in the blue suite across from you."

Edward motioned the captain to follow him. "Come, Stewart. Darcy and my mother keep the gentlemen and the ladies in different wings of the house. I will show you the way."

As they all disappeared to different reaches of the house, including the countess and Georgiana, Darcy remained staring off at the point where the lady, who had quite literally sent his heart pounding in a manner he had never experienced previously, had disappeared. Growing up together, Darcy had, most assuredly, idolized his older cousin, for Edward had always appeared stronger and wiser than he, but, until a few moments prior, he thought he had finally caught up to the man; perhaps, even, had outdistanced him in many of the essentials required of an English gentleman. Yet, with absolute certainty, his cousin had once again left Darcy wishing for some "unknown," which Fitzwilliam possessed.

* * *

Twice more that afternoon, Darcy and the countess had welcomed guests to Pemberley. As if nothing unusual had occurred earlier, neither of them uttered a word regarding the colonel's announcement.

Between the arrival of Miss Davidson and her brother, both long time Derbyshire acquaintances of Georgiana and another pair of brothers and sisters, Mr. Whalen, a casual friend of Darcy from his university days, and the man's sister, Miss Whalen, Darcy had made his way to the nursery to peer in on Miss Bennet's progress with Hursts' boys, who he, personally, thought could use a firmer hand on their shoulders.

He peeked into the rooms set aside for the nursery to watch Miss Bennet set soldier figures on a map of Europe that he recognized as once belonging to him, at a time when Mr. Sheffield had been his tutor, rather than his valet. Instantly, an image of one of his favorite memories of his mother came rushing in. Lady Anne Darcy was sprawled out upon the nursery room floor playing pirate with him as she assembled a stack of boxes to provide him a hiding place. Since Cassandra's birth, he had often thought he wished to replicate such moments with his child. He almost ached from the knowledge that Anne would never be able to see their child grow into womanhood.

"This, Horace, is the French leader, Bonaparte." Miss Bennet placed the figure on the map. "What did we learn a moment ago regarding how the English commander, the Duke of Wellington—" She paused to touch a soldier painted with a redcoat. ". . . managed to outmaneuver the French at Waterloo?"

The boy looked to Miss Bennet with a bit of awe before responding. "Wellington's men used the constant rain as their partner during the battle."

"I know. I know," his brother chimed in. "Old Boney could not move his heavy guns in the rain."

The lady placed a comforting hand on the child to draw his attention to her lesson. "Excellent response from both of you, but, please remember, Philip, a gentleman would not speak of his enemy with a derogatory term. We agreed to call the French commander by his proper name."

Darcy would disagree with her statement, but he knew the boy's tutor would likely reward the child with a slap on the back of his hand, instead of the touch of comfort the lady supplied. Her gentle prompting might save the child a harder lesson to learn.

"I am sorry, Miss Bennet." Philip dropped his chin in what appeared to be honest regret.

"Nothing major of which to be sorry," she assured. "Just remember, young gentlemen must always speak well. People will judge you with first impressions, and you wish those judgements to be in your favor."

"When may we finish setting up the battlefield?" Horace asked.

Miss Bennet smiled on the boys. "If you have a steady hand, we might do the deed now so you may consider your strategies before I return in the morning."

"May we play soldier with a few of the red and blue ones until you return?"

She glanced up to notice Darcy standing in the open door and smiled. He thought her smile could prove quite addictive.

"I did not mean to disturb you, Miss Bennet. I thought I might steal a few moments with my daughter." He, most assuredly, came regularly to the nursery to spend time with his child, but such was not his purpose on this occasion. He wanted to ease his mind regarding the Hursts' abuse of Miss Bennet's goodness.

"I believe Miss Cassandra is asleep," she said softly. "Mrs. Anderson slipped down to the kitchen for fresh tea. I told her I would remain until her return."

"Teaching the boys something of Waterloo, I see," he remarked as he entered the nursery.

She glanced to the array of toy soldiers before her. "The boys and I agree we could enjoy playing while learning something of England's history, although, in reality, I suppose some of our men should be wearing green like the French chasseurs." A blush caressed her cheeks. "As I have tended young ladies for the last four years, I fear my historical studies have been placed aside for more feminine attributes."

"You studied history?" he asked, curious about this particular woman.

"Not formally, but my father was a great reader of a variety of topics, which he shared with any of his daughters who cared to learn more." Her smile widened. "As I was his favorite, we spent countless hours reading and dissecting passages full of history, science, the classics, and the like."

31

Darcy stepped further into the room. "I possess an extensive library at Pemberley. If you wish to partake of reading, do so to your heart's content."

Tears misted her eyes. "Truly, you do not mind, sir? Your generosity is a lovely gift." An idea found her as she glanced again to the two boys who shoved first one soldier forward and then the next while making sounds of combat. "Might you possess any pieces on the battles of the most recent war? The boys and I could read them together and act out the battles on the map with the soldiers."

"I will pull a few books which might prove beneficial and ask Mr. Nathan to deliver them to your quarters. If you have no objections, I will add a tome on the Jacobites. My cousin Edward and I always enjoyed acting out the bloodiest of the battles." He smiled in memory. "The colonel would be pleased to share his interest in the rebellion. I am certain my cousin has spoken of his deep interest in history."

Her face took on a puzzled look. "I cannot say Colonel Fitzwilliam and I have held a long enough acquaintance to have shared such memories."

Chapter four

A maid directed Elizabeth along a passage to what was supposed to be her quarters, but she shook her head in denial. "Pardon." She reached out and touched the girl's shoulder. "Susan, is it?"

"Yes, miss." Elizabeth prided herself on learning names quickly. In her line of employment, remembering names eased her way into the "hierarchy" of the servants.

"I do not wish to sound critical, but there must be some mistake. This section of the house appears to be designed for Mr. Darcy's important guests."

"It is, miss."

Elizabeth swallowed her concern. "Then I should not be housed with the other guests," she said politely.

The maid frowned. "I don't understand, miss. Lady Matlock specifically set aside this very room for you. Mrs. Reynolds asked me, she did, to escort you here." She reached for the latch and set it free, allowing the door to swing wide.

Elizabeth glanced to the room to view Hannah standing in the middle of the space. "Is it not somethin' to behold, Miss Bennet?"

Elizabeth turned to the other maid. "I beg you pardon, Susan, I was mistaken. If you will please present Mrs. Reynolds my best regards, I would appreciate it. I shall do the same with the countess and Mr. Darcy. Thank you for your patience with me."

The girl looked oddly upon Elizabeth, but she nodded her understanding and scurried away.

Elizabeth stepped into the elegant room and reverently closed the door. She squeezed her eyes shut and breathed in deeply the lovely clean fragrance filling the space. An ache of recognition brought tears rushing to her eyes. "*Lavender*," she thought. "*At Longbourn, Mrs. Hill always made certain there was dried lavender in my room.*"

She opened her eyes to find Hannah studying her intently. "Do you feel under the weather, miss?"

Elizabeth shook off the idea. "I was just enjoying the moment." She grinned widely at the maid. "One of us has been excessively Godly of late for us to be so blessed. I must assume it has been you, for, I admit to possessing ill thoughts against my former employer. Therefore, I am most fortunate the colonel found a saint to accompany me to Derbyshire."

Hannah laughed easily. "I be called many things in my life, miss, but a 'saint' not be among them." She returned to her tasks. "I did not know what you wished to wear to supper, but I took the liberty of takin' an iron to both the blue wool and the green cotton."

"You are very good to me. I have enjoyed your company on our travels."

"And I you, miss. I never thought to be servin' a fine lady."

Elizabeth quickly denied the maid's statement. "I am but a governess, Hannah. A servant, just as you are."

Hannah frowned deeply. "You may have fallen on hard times, but you be a superior lady, nonetheless. You've fine manners, but, more importantly, you've a good heart."

Elizabeth felt herself tearing up again. "When must you leave me?"

"If'n it pleases you, miss, Mrs. Reynolds said I could come and go as you saw fit." Hannah dropped her chin in obvious indecision. "I be thinkin', like you, if'n I could prove myself useful, mayhap there be a position for me at Pemberley, and I not be needin' to return to Gloucestershire and the inn. I could see me family regular."

Elizabeth knew she frowned, but she held more than a few concerns regarding Hannah's suggestion. "I believe we must speak to Colonel Fitzwilliam first before any arrangements can be made for a permanent position. The colonel has offered to see to your return to Gloucestershire at the end of Christmastide. He made no offer of employment beyond the festive days, nor can the colonel speak of employment within Mr. Darcy's home."

Hannah appeared concern. "My father would not wish me to offend Mr. Darcy."

Elizabeth squeezed the back of Hannah's hand in comfort. "Let us accept Mrs. Reynolds's suggestion that you come and go for the first week or so. While at Pemberley, make yourself useful with chores in the kitchen or cleaning the rooms set aside for guests. In truth, I have little need for a dresser, so you should have plenty of time to prove yourself worthy. Meanwhile, when the opportunity arrives, I shall speak privately to Colonel Fitzwilliam and determine his opinion on whether we should approach Mr. Darcy or not. For all we know, Mr. Darcy may have no need of another maid or you could be exactly for what he has been searching."

* * *

"Good," Lady Matlock said when she entered Darcy's study unannounced. "I was hoping you would be down early. Did you have an opportunity to speak to Fitzwilliam?"

Darcy had come down after dressing, for he was still troubled by his brief conversation with Miss Bennet and a longer exchange with his cousin. The pair appeared to be only mildly fond of each other, but he could not name the reason why he found this promising. "Did you also discuss Miss Bennet with your son?"

"I did," she said, claiming a seat before Darcy's desk before he had an opportunity to do more than rise to greet her properly. Such was a true indication of her agitation, for his Aunt Matlock always paused for necessary niceties expected for one in her position.

"And?" Darcy asked.

"I am nearly as confused now as I was previously."

"As am I," he admitted. "Share with me what you learned. Then we can compare the colonel's tales. It is not like Fitzwilliam to present either of us a Banbury tale; yet, I am more than a little troubled by how quickly this relationship with Miss Bennet has formed."

"Agreed." The countess's frown lines deepened. "Edward spoke of how Lord Newland's son took upon himself a too fond of a liking to Miss Bennet. We know how some men use their power over

35

those they employ." Darcy nodded his head in agreement: The idea bothered Darcy, but he held his tongue, for such was not their purpose in this meeting, and time was short. The supper bell would ring soon. "Apparently," his aunt continued, "one evening recently, while deep in his cups, Lieutenant Newland accosted the lady. The lieutenant chased Miss Bennet down the stairs, lost his balance, tumbled, and fell, breaking one leg in two places."

"I received fewer details, but the story was essentially the same," Darcy confirmed. "Do we know whether Fitzwilliam held the lady's acquaintance before encountering her at Newland Hall?"

"My son did not speak to the length of their ac00qfuaintance, but he has been with the Newlands for a fortnight. Not an ideal period for an affection to form between him and the lady, but, most assuredly, possible. Matlock says he knew we would marry in less than a month's acquaintance."

Darcy said with mixed emotions, "My father always said he knew he would marry my mother after they had danced together but once—the matter of half an hour."

Lady Matlock simply sighed as all women do when speaking of affairs of the heart, before she continued. "From what the colonel said, Fitzwilliam had warned Newland away from the lady several times before the fall occurred. Even so, when he defended Miss Bennet against Lady Newland's allegations of the young woman being a strumpet and only out to become the new viscountess, the colonel and Lady Newland exchanged a string of recriminations, many of which I shall address to her ladyship when next we meet in London. No one speaks to my son as such without receiving a direct cut from the Matlocks. His lordship will also have a few words with Lord Newland about the man taking his wife in hand or being ostracized by all."

"I never cared for the woman," Darcy said.

The countess shrugged off her moment of pique regarding Lady Newland. "Fitzwilliam decided it would be best for Captain Stewart and him to learn where Miss Bennet would land next. Although my son did not say the words, I have the feeling Lady Newland's expulsion forced my Edward's hand in this matter. He could not permit Miss Bennet to be set adrift without his acting."

Although Darcy attempted to hide the flicker of hope that Miss Bennet was not meant for his cousin, he asked, "Is it possible then, that the pair are not betrothed?"

The countess shook off Darcy's notion, dashing his quickly formed aspirations. "I specifically asked if he and the young lady held an understanding, and the colonel confirmed that they did."

"I see," Darcy said in serious tones. "Then, if Miss Bennet is the colonel's choice of wife, we should lend him our support. I have had only two brief conversations with the lady, but I found nothing objectionable beyond her loss of circumstances. If you had observed how well she had taken Hursts' boys under her control and how she was teaching them something of Wellington's history while she entertained them, you would feel easier about the woman."

The countess sat in quiet contemplation for a few minutes. "I want my son to know happiness: For years, Fitzwilliam has viewed the worst of humanity; he deserves someone who will recognize the fact he may struggle more than he cares for others to know."

Darcy swallowed the tightness forming in his throat, as he considered Edward's fragility as being something quite real. He had always thought of his cousin as invincible, but it seemed others saw something in the man that Darcy had not permitted himself to view. Was it because he frequently questioned his own reason that he did not veer from the lot cast for each of them? "We do not know enough of Miss Bennet to determine whether she is such a woman."

The countess sucked in a quick breath. "No, we do not, but I intend to learn for myself if the lady is worthy of my son or not, and I pray you will join me in discovering whether the young woman has decided to hitch her hopes to the earldom or whether she holds our Edward in affection."

In the distance, the bell rang in the main hall, signaling that supper would be served in half an hour. Darcy rose to escort his aunt to the drawing room where their guests would gather to wait. "We will safeguard the colonel's happiness with our vigilance, and, if the lady's emotions are not as engaged as are your son's, we will find her another position and send her on her way."

"Find her another position?" the countess asked. "If Miss Bennet proves false, why would I wish to assist her?"

Darcy did not look at his aunt as he designed his response; instead, he directed their steps toward the door. "I am not best pleased with how Lady Newland treated Miss Bennet. Perhaps the lady simply agreed to the colonel's offer, for she had no place else to turn. Without a letter of character, she is not likely to find a comparable, or, even a better, position. Mayhap a reference from one of us will be all that is required to have her abandon the hope of being part of Matlock's family."

"Will Miss Bennet not develop a taste of luxury and not wish to step aside now that she holds the golden key?"

Darcy leaned his head to the side to speak privately as others waited for them at the bottom of the stairs. "I trust the colonel's opinions as deeply as I do my own. Moreover, if the young lady is only thinking of being a Fitzwilliam, she would not have announced the fact that she has been employed as a governess, nor would she have spent two hours entertaining Hurst's children."

"Are you certain, Darcy?" she asked from the corner of her mouth.

He paused casually to lift her fingers to his lips in a show of affection while he whispered, "Mrs. Reynolds reports Miss Bennet protested the exquisite quarters set aside for her. If she were set on a position in a prominent family, she would have simply accepted the 'luxury,' as you term it, for what it is. I am more inclined to believe she possesses a loyalty to the colonel. Unfortunately, at this time, I cannot yet say whether that loyalty is a deep affection or not. Even so, I imagine, between the two of us, we will discover the truth of the matter before the colonel commits himself to a manipulator."

"Yes, we will. Of that, I have no doubt," the countess declared.

* * *

As they went in to supper, Darcy caught his cousin's arm. "If you hold no objection, I think it best we do not speak of Miss Bennet's situation and your agreement with the others, if that is acceptable to you?"

The colonel glanced ahead to where the lady in question entered the supper room on the arm of Captain Stewart. "I understand," the colonel said, while a frown marked his forehead. "It will be necessary for me to warn Stewart, but you should know Hurst is already suggesting that Miss Bennet should by employed by 'you' to tend 'his' children. It was generous of the lady to offer her assistance, but I did not escort her to Pemberley to work for the likes of a lazy son of—. Well, you know what I think of the man. I wished you and her ladyship to take Miss Bennet's acquaintance and learn more of how exceptional she is."

Darcy fought hard not to permit his frown from joining his cousin's "Naturally, the countess and I wish to learn more of the lady," he assured.

The colonel set their steps in motion, tugging Darcy along beside him. "Promise me you will not permit the countess her attempts to intimidate Miss Bennet. You will remain close to the countess. The lady had enough ill treatment with the Newlands. Although I know mother possesses a softer side than most would think, she was born with an air of superiority that she wields as if it were a sword when least we expect it."

Darcy paused briefly to respond. "If it makes you feel better, Lady Matlock is determined to seek out Miss Bennet's finer qualities."

* * *

Once the ladies had withdrawn from the supper hall, Captain Stewart asked, "Do you suppose the weather will hold for some shooting tomorrow morning, Darcy? The colonel seems to think we could enjoy a bit of sport while at Pemberley."

"According to my land steward, who is rarely wrong about these things, we will have snow by week's end, but I imagine you should know some success tomorrow. I will ask Mr. Stanley to have runners available, as well as the dogs. I assume you mean to shoot birds, rather than rabbits."

Bingley, Mr. Davidson, and Mr. Whalen expressed a desire to join Captain Stewart. Hurst declined rising early to join the gentlemen.

"You will join us, Colonel, will you not?" Mr. Whalen asked.

Edward shot a glance to Darcy. "I told Miss Darcy I would spend some time with her before the day became too busy. What say you, Darcy? Will Georgiana mind if I enjoy some sport with the gentlemen first? We should return by mid-morning."

Darcy shrugged. "One would think that after all this time I would be an expert on my sister's disposition, but I hold no insights worth knowing regarding the feminine mind. Miss Darcy, however, I will say, is, generally, a reasonable young lady. It is not as if you intend to abandon her for more than a few hours, and you do plan to remain at Pemberley until Twelfth Night, do you not?"

"I overheard my sister and Miss Whalen asking Miss Darcy if they might all go into the village tomorrow," Mr. Davidson informed the men.

The colonel told Stewart, "I will speak to my young cousin and ask if we might change the hour of our conversation. If Georgiana does not mind, I would be happy to join you for some sport. We did not have the opportunity for the exercise while at Newland Hall."

Darcy stood to signal it was time to leave. "Might we rejoin the ladies?"

The colonel stated the obvious. "I did not hear you speak your willingness to join the gentlemen, Darcy."

"I scheduled the tenant hearings early so they would not interfere with the supper and the ball the countess has planned after St. Stephen's Day. My aunt was most specific on my responsibilities to the event," he said with a smile.

His cousin jovially claimed a hold on Darcy's shoulder. "Be careful, Darcy. By Twelfth Night, the Countess of Matlock will spoil you with her expert management, making it impossible for you to claim a second wife."

"Trust me," Darcy said with a grin. "I will not be seeking another wife any time soon."

Chapter five

Darcy took up a place near the fireplace, not because he was chilled by the evening's cold, rather, because he wished to observe his guests, especially Miss Bennet and the colonel. He thought it very telling that his cousin did not join his "supposed" betrothed, who was in an animated conversation with the countess. Instead, Edward and the captain had joined Georgiana, Miss Davidson, and Miss Whalen. Bingley, Mr. Whalen, and Mr. Davidson, along with Hurst, enjoyed a game of cards, while Miss Bingley and Mrs. Hurst had their heads together, likely to criticize all in the room.

When they had entered the room, Mr. Davidson initially had escorted Georgiana to the bench before the pianoforte. The man had been very solicitous of Darcy's sister, a fact that had not gone unnoticed by Darcy. He was thankful Georgiana no longer avoided the company of young gentlemen of her age, although, in truth, neither Davidson or Whalen would be Darcy's first choice of a husband for his sister. Whalen was closer to Darcy's age, and Darcy thought Davidson required four or five years in the world to know the type of maturity, in Darcy's opinion, a married man required.

He had thought himself prepared to guide Anne's steps away from his wife's dependence on her mother, Lady Catherine de Bourgh. Unfortunately, he now knew, even if Anne had not passed from childbed fever, she, likely, would never have been capable of running Pemberley as its mistress. She was too timid. Too uninterested in her home estate. And, although he had never spoken of his opinion of his late wife to others, Darcy considered Anne too weak-minded to embrace the changes barreling down on the landed

41

gentry and too ill-suited to rise above what would likely be a major change in the status quo.

"A quid for your thoughts," Miss Bingley stood close at his side. He had been so engrossed in his belated consideration of Anne's unsuitability that he had taken no note of Miss Bingley's rise from her place beside her sister to join him. If he had, Darcy would have been on the move to avoid her. He made a mental note to corner Bingley tomorrow and express his disdain of Bingley's family's assumption that they could attend events Bingley did. Their audacity was likely the reason Bingley had yet to discover a woman of gentry who would marry him. What woman, even one whose family could use the fortune Bingley brought to the table, would want to be constantly in the company of those hanging on to the fringes of society by their fingernails? Darcy should have already expressed his dismay to his friend, but Miss Bennet's unexpected entrance earlier today had thrown Darcy off his agenda.

"I fear, all that entertains me," he said evenly and with a touch of coldness in his tone, "is whether my guests are enjoying their evening at Pemberley."

She followed his eyes when they returned to Miss Bennet's fine countenance. He wished he could look away from the woman; yet, he took such great personal pleasure in studying her, that his eyes returned again and again, as if he had no control, which was another issue altogether.

"Who is she?" Miss Bingley asked.

Darcy could easily hear the derision in her tone. "An 'invited' guest in my house," he replied crisply.

She looked up at him; remarkably, no chagrin marked her features. "I know she arrived with Colonel Fitzwilliam and Captain Stewart, but what is her lineage? Who are her family? I heard someone say she was a governess. What might Colonel Fitzwilliam mean by exposing the rest of your guests to such a woman?"

There had been a time when Darcy "tolerated" Bingley's sisters for his friend's sake, but in the time he had been married to Anne, he had never invited any of the Bingleys to Pemberley—not because he wished to sever ties with Bingley himself, but, rather, because of Anne's fragile social nature. Miss Bingley and Mrs. Hurst would have done to Anne what they had previously done to Georgiana. They would have smiled and patted Anne's hand while all along looking for a means to bring her down or to use Anne to better their position in society.

"What does the colonel mean by exposing you and the others to the daughter of a gentleman—a woman well read in a variety of subjects?" Darcy quipped. "Perhaps Fitzwilliam meant to give his family the acquaintance of a woman who had earned his respect."

"Yet, a governess?" she chastised. "Surely you do not approve."

"Your disdain for others is an unbecoming habit you should abandon, Miss Bingley," he stated coldly. "Everyone in this room is just as likely to fall upon hard times as the next. Our country and our economy are on a great precipice and which way it will plunge could mean the success or failure of our great nation. You could easily be in the same situation as Miss Bennet if Bingley's business interests take a turn for the worse. Do not throw rocks at others. God has a way of bringing the prideful to their knees." He paused briefly to calm his anger. "I do not wish to be cruel, but you present me little choice. In the eyes of society, even with her diminished circumstances, Miss Bennet's place in society still outranks a woman whose fortune is based on trade."

Miss Bingley went pale under his speaking gaze. "I was not aware your disposition had changed so dramatically with your marriage, Mr. Darcy," she said on a rasp.

"I admit, in the past, I permitted my familial pride free rein, for I did not wish to offend, and, quite truthfully, I, like you, thought my world would go on and on without disruption. However, take note of this, in essentials I am very much the man I always was, Miss Bingley. For this evening and the future, let us simply agree that in 'my' house, I may entertain whoever I choose. If this idea distresses you, I will ask Mr. Nathan to send to the coach house and have Mr. Hurst's carriage prepared for your immediate departure." He bowed stiffly. "Pardon me, I must speak to the countess before Miss Darcy chooses another piece to perform. I never miss the opportunity to enjoy my sister's brilliance."

* * *

The supper had been exceedingly handsome, and there had been all the servants and articles of plate that Elizabeth had assumed would be set before her. She could not help but to consider the delight her mother would have had in viewing her second daughter being greeted by a countess, of all things. Mrs. Bennet's "nerves" would have been on full display for all to have observed, and Elizabeth would have known great happiness to have presented her mother such delight.

The thought of what could have been had nearly brought Elizabeth to tears as she glanced about the table. Despite Mrs. Bennet's rancor, Elizabeth understood her mother's anger. Elizabeth's refusal of Mr. Collins's addresses had doomed them all to a life of penury. Often, she cursed herself for her stubbornness and wondered if it had not been better if she had sacrificed her future for the sake of her mother and sisters; yet, at the time, they had all thought, at least she had thought, there would be time for her sisters and her to find husbands, perhaps not as rich as Mr. Darcy—her heart sighed, for she imagined her host was even richer than Lord Matlock, but, most assuredly, they would have claimed suitable matches.

Then, her dearest papa had passed, without warning, and had left Elizabeth with more regrets than she could pronounce.

She had, generally, kept her own company throughout the meal, not engaging, but, instead, observing the others.

However, when the ladies returned to the drawing room, she set both her shoulders and her mind into relaxing. When the countess asked her to sit with her, Elizabeth claimed the opportunity to win her ladyship's loyalty in hopes of a recommendation from the countess when Elizabeth departed Pemberley.

Once they were settled, Lady Matlock said, "Darcy tells me your father was a gentleman from the southern shires."

"Yes, my lady. We resided in Hertfordshire," Elizabeth shared.

"How long has it been since your father passed?" she asked softly.

Elizabeth swallowed the emotions that always plagued her when she considered the chaos that ensued after Mr. Bennet had collapsed. "Nearly five years, ma'am."

"You have been on your own for that long? You must have been quite young to take on so much responsibility."

"Only twenty at the time," she said softly.

"And there was no one to whom you could turn?"

Elizabeth sighed deeply. She had been called on often to answer that particular question. "My sisters and I number five. My Aunt and Uncle Phillips took my mother and two youngest sisters in with them. Meanwhile, Aunt and Uncle Gardiner brought two of my sisters and me to London to live with them. Although they did not ask it of me, I immediately searched for employment."

"Are you the eldest?" Lady Matlock asked, her brows crinkling in apparent disapproval.

"No, ma'am, the second."

"Why did not the eldest seek out employment first?" she demanded.

"I could not have permitted Jane to assume such responsibilities. Our Jane, you see, has the face and the disposition of an angel. The children in many homes would have taken advantage of Jane's goodness, and I doubt many gentlemen could not look upon her . . ."

"And not act in a manner comparable to Lieutenant Newland?" The countess finished Elizabeth's thoughts.

Elizabeth dropped the subject. "Essentially, it was my fault my family suffered," she admitted. "It should have been me who was banished from the comfort provided by my Uncle Gardiner."

"How so?" the countess inquired.

Elizabeth lowered her voice. "I had the opportunity to save them all. You see, my father's heir offered me his hand in marriage, but I refused him. My mother lamented my decision, claiming I would drive them all into the hedgerows."

Lady Matlock's eyebrow rose in obvious curiosity. "May I ask why you refused a man who could have saved your family?"

"If you had ever taken the gentleman's acquaintance, you would understand," Elizabeth said with a grin.

The countess barked a laugh. "The type of man who has a woman becoming a fishwife or a murderess?"

Elizabeth smiled easily and relaxed a fraction. "Exactly."

45

* * *

Darcy thought it quite odd that Miss Bennet never once looked to Colonel Fitzwilliam with any longing apparent in her expression nor did she appear to express a desire to join the others at the instrument. Unable to stifle his curiosity completely, at length, he joined the countess and Miss Bennet by moving one of the nearby chairs closer to where they sat.

"Might I claim my share of your conversation?" he asked as he sat.

His aunt looked up and smiled. "Miss Bennet and I were discussing the casualties in an unequal marriage."

The fact his aunt sported an actual smile and not the one the countess employed when speaking to someone in polite disapproval was encouraging; yet, Darcy wondered if his aunt had broached the subject of a possible marriage between the son of an earl and an impoverished gentlewoman.

"What is your opinion, Miss Bennet, of an unequal marriage?" he asked in what he hoped were casual tones.

"Does your question ask of 'unequal' in depth of affection or in social standing?" she inquired with a challenging lift of her brows.

"Both," he replied. "Either of interest to you?"

"A dear friend of mine once offered me sage advice on the topic," she clarified. "Although I advocate greedily for those involved to be permitted their privacy, I can easily understand how a lady, or perhaps a gentleman, who possesses both a great strength of feeling and a composure of temper, along with a uniform cheerfulness of manner, could appear to those not of an intimate acquaintance as being impertinent and uncaring.

"My friend often argued that it is sometimes a disadvantage to be so very guarded. She reasoned that if a woman conceals her affection with the same skill from the object of it, she may lose the opportunity of fixing the gentleman, and it will then be but poor consolation to believe the world equally in the dark. There is so much of gratitude or vanity in almost every attachment, that it is not safe to leave any to itself."

"Do you not think," the countess countered, "we all begin freely—a slight preference is natural enough, but there are few of us who have heart enough to be really in love without encouragement?"

Darcy heard his aunt's doubts loud and clear in her question. He, too, could not conceive of a match between the colonel and the lady, not because neither was undesirable, but because, in his estimation, Miss Bennet was too "desirable" to be ignored, and his cousin continued to ignore the lady.

"You suggest," Miss Bennet contended, "that a woman should show more affection than she feels. Is that a correct assumption?"

The countess pressed her point. "If a lady does not help the gentleman on, the man may never do more than like her."

Again, Darcy heard his aunt reasoning out how Miss Bennet had managed to attract the colonel enough to draw forth a proposal, especially as many others had attempted to "trap" Fitzwilliam and failed. Whether he said the words aloud or not, Darcy wondered if his cousin's heart was engaged or whether the colonel had spoken a proposal to save Miss Bennet's tattered reputation.

Miss Bennet argued, "Should not the gentleman find it out, especially, if the woman makes no endeavor to conceal it?" She glanced about the room. "Despite my holding no more than a speaking acquaintance with any in this room, I can view, quite easily, Miss Whalen's apparent interest in Mr. Davidson, Miss Bingley's designs on Mr. Darcy, and Miss Darcy's pining for the colonel's attentions."

Darcy's eyes swept the room to find Miss Bingley's resting on his person. Instead of denying the lady's assumptions regarding Miss Bingley, he said, "I was not aware of Miss Whalen's hopes for Mr. Davidson's attentions, although theirs would be a joining of two distinguished families." Had he not thought, only a quarter hour earlier, that Mr. Davidson's interest rested in Georgiana? Darcy hoped what Miss Bennet described was not true, for his sister and Miss Whalen had long been friends. As to her comment about Georgiana's interest, he wondered if Miss Bennet could not be jealous of Georgiana. "As to the colonel's relationship with my sister, Fitzwilliam serves, along with me, as Miss Darcy's guardian. They are family and very close."

She glanced again to the grouping gathered around the pianoforte. "As you say, sir," she repeated, but Darcy held the distinct impression the lady possessed her doubts. "As to Miss Whalen, I would say if nothing is in question but the desire to be married, then the lady should secure the young gentleman as quickly as possible, for there will be leisure for their falling in love as much as she chooses. Mayhap, if I were determined to name a rich husband, or, any husband, I dare say, I might consider adopting such a plan. One cannot be a critic under such circumstances."

"As you describe such a courtship," Darcy asserted, "the pair might know nothing more of each other than the fact the gentleman possesses a hearty appetite, enjoys shooting, and employs a competent valet. Whereas, he might realize the lady blushes easily and they both prefer Vingt-et-un to Commerce, but with respect to any other leading characteristic, I do not imagine that much has been unfolded."

Miss Bennet acknowledged the truth of his words with a simple nod of her head. "If Mr. Davidson is Miss Whalen's desire, with all my heart, I wish her success, and if she married the gentleman tomorrow, I should think the lady possessed as good a chance at happiness as if she were to be studying his character for a twelve month period. In my most humble opinion, happiness in marriage is entirely a matter of chance. It appears to me that if the dispositions of the parties are ever so well-known to each other, or ever so similar beforehand, it does not advance their felicity in the least. They will always continue to grow sufficiently unlike afterward to have their share of vexation, and it is better to know as little as possible of the defects of the person with whom one is to pass his or her life."

The countess must have heard more than either of them cared to acknowledge, for she quickly turned the conversation to how his tenant hearings were progressing. Within minutes, Miss Bennet claimed fatigue and asked to be excused so she might rest in her quarters.

Once the lady had left the room, Darcy quickly switched his seat to sit beside his aunt. Softly, he asked, "Do you think the lady believes all she shared? Even though she speaks to what appears to be the opposite to her verbalized stance about the need for a coming together of hearts in marriage, such leaves me with the opinion she would prefer to marry where affection is evident. If such is so, would the lady consider marrying a rich man and learn to love the fellow afterwards?" He was asking his question as much for himself as he was for Fitzwilliam.

"I am not certain the lady holds a definite opinion. Miss Bennet argued both for the idea of marrying for love, as well as marrying for security. I do not believe she holds a true idea of the commitment she has made to my son. That being said, I admit I do not hold such against her; few women have ample opportunities to learn truly the nature of the character of the man whose hand she has accepted."

Darcy asked, "What else did you learn of the lady?"

The countess glanced quickly around the room to be certain no one could overhear their exchange. "Miss Bennet's decision not to marry her father's heir is what sent the family into penury. The lady blames herself for their current situation. She refused the comfort of extended family to set out on her journey as a governess as a sort of penance for her supposed 'crimes.'"

"And your opinion?" he asked as a bit of pride in Miss Bennet's determination found a place in his heart. He knew few ladies who would have acted so bravely under the circumstances.

"The lady does not complain about her lot in life, but she regrets that her choices affected her family. Even so, Miss Bennet does not regret her refusal of the man's hand beyond the separation of her family, scattered among the homes of relations. She openly admits she could not have well tolerated a simpleton, as she describes her father's heir." The countess lowered her voice, "I sometimes wonder, if Anne had not passed in delivering your daughter, how well you two would have gone on together without disdain being made known. Lady Catherine long thought you and Anne equals, but our Anne was a weak, timid woman, possessing little understanding and learning. I agreed that you had little choice, but the family did you a disservice in allowing your marriage to proceed. I have spoken to Matlock often of our failing you."

Darcy simply nodded his acceptance. Like Miss Bennet, he held his regrets regarding his marriage, but, also, like the lady, he would spend the remainder of his days questioning his decision.

The countess continued, "At least Miss Bennet did not appear concerned over Edward spending no time at her side this evening."

"Perhaps such is part of their arrangement," Darcy suggested. "Surely, the colonel knew we would wish some private time to learn more of the lady, and they have purposely chosen not to alert the others to their understanding. We have until the end of Christmastide to provide the colonel our opinion of his choice."

The countess glanced to where Fitzwilliam joined the others in singing a song that Georgiana played. "My initial analysis is I hold no objection to Miss Bennet, other than the lady's reduced circumstances. My son, most assuredly, could have chosen someone not in possession of the lady's good sense."

* * *

As she crawled into bed that evening, Elizabeth considered the perfection of her day. Despite being a governess by trade, she had been welcomed into the home of Mr. Darcy of Pemberley and had dined and conversed with the Countess of Matlock. Even dressed in a drab, well-worn gown, her opinions had been sought out and debated as if they held true merit. Moreover, throughout the day, Mr. Darcy had sought her company, even going so far as to place her hand on his arm, never once showing disdain for her impoverishment. "And this room is so large," she murmured into the stillness. "It is large enough that sharing it with both Jane and Mary would be no great discomfort."

She silently wished her elder sisters could observe her in this moment, for not only would they doubt the magnitude of her good fortune, but, Elizabeth knew, they, too, deserved such a moment— deserved not to be considered less than what they were: the daughters of a country gentleman and worthy of a few moments of dignity. "I miss Jane and Mary more than words can express," she told the empty room.

Elizabeth permitted herself to relive each of her "adventures" today from the time she stepped down from Captain Stewart's well-cushioned carriage to a few moments earlier when Hannah tucked her into bed. She would savor those memories and any yet to come and add them to her happy recollections of the time before her father's passing to relive again and again while she toiled in loneliness and self-isolation at her next post. Before coming to Pemberley, Elizabeth had nearly forgotten how much she adored the company of others

"And Mr. Darcy's smile," she told the night as she blew out the candle. "The smile on the lips of the most handsome gentleman I have ever beheld. Definitely more handsome than even Mr. Wickham," she giggled. "And well worth remembering. Along with this unexpected holiday, likely the last one I shall ever know."

* * *

Although he had excused his valet, Mr. Sheffield, a half hour prior, Darcy still paced the room from one end to the other. His mind was full of the very enticing Miss Bennet. Just closing his eyes, he could easily draw forth the image of the lady, with her enchanting smile and exceedingly fine eyes. "What am I doing?"

He paused to look out upon the frost-covered lawn below. "The morning shall prove perfect for shooting. It is a shame you cannot go with the other gentlemen." The idea only served to bring Darcy back to the crux of his dilemma. "Faith and true, I know no finer gentleman than my cousin," he stated in firm tones, hoping to instill that idea in his heart, as well as his head. "My cousin—the man who has earned Miss Bennet's affections.

"A slim possibility exists that the lady's intention is to improve her situation, and, if such is true, might Miss Bennet easily switch her affections to any of the gentlemen in attendance? Bingley's head, for example, was always easily turned by a handsome countenance, and my friend has more than four thousand a year. Moreover, Bingley's fortune comes from trade, lacking the impediments the other gentlemen and I know all too well. Both would win: Miss Bennet would achieve a higher status in society, and Bingley would marry into a gentleman's family, providing him a leg up." Yet, Darcy did not want the lady to turn her attentions to Bingley or any of the others. He wanted her for his own. "However, the lady speaks only of her loyalty to my cousin.

"And there is the rub," Darcy confessed. "Although a fine gentleman, my cousin cannot be sincerely involved with the lady, not

51

that Fitzwilliam could not appreciate Miss Bennet's finer qualities, but, rather, the idea of marriage is a foreign one to the colonel. Unfortunately, for me, the lady would please me quite well, except for the fact I am a most terrible sort of gent. The lady will soon be my cousin by marriage, and I desire her for my own. I must firmly place my jealousy behind me and wish them both happiness. No other choice lies before you, Darcy," he told his heart. "Miss Bennet will soon be Mrs. Fitzwilliam, daughter in marriage to the Earl of Matlock."

Chapter six

Monday, 21 December 1818

Darcy had seen the other gentlemen off early in the morning, pleasantly surprised that Bingley had roused out Hurst, whose indolence never ceased to disappoint.

"Georgiana," he said in surprise when he spotted his sister exiting her rooms in the family wing. "I am a bit amazed to find you up so early. In truth, I have missed looking upon your fine countenance each day. Your presence always seems to set my day aright."

She glanced around, almost as if she were nervous. "I suppose it is quite gauche of me to appear below stairs when it is customary for the men to have the morning room to themselves and we women to take our breakfast in our quarters during a house party." She ran her handkerchief through her fingers, which was a telling sign of her apparent agitation.

"Nonsense," he pronounced. "Pemberley is your home. Just because the countess has deemed it the right of men to have the morning room to themselves does not change the fact that Pemberley is your home, and, if you wish to break your fast in the morning room, then do so. We set our own rules at Pemberley, and I will speak to the countess on the matter. No one says only the gentlemen have a right to hot dishes on the sideboard, and having the women, who choose to do so, to join us, would provide more staff to tend to baths and laundry and such."

She nodded her head in acceptance.

"Might I escort you below?" he asked, presenting her his arm. "I have missed having you by my side."

She politely placed her hand on his arm, and Darcy dutifully turned their steps toward the lower level. They were just about to descend when Georgiana provided him a true indication of her purpose this morning. "I suppose our cousin chose to join the other gentlemen this morning," she said softly.

Darcy eyed her suspiciously. "You are well aware that the colonel is not one to lie abed half the morning, and he, most devotedly, enjoys his sport." He paused to look upon her with "new" eyes. "I thought Fitzwilliam spoke to you about his joining the men. He assured me he would do so."

"He did," she said with downcast eyes. "I was simply hoping—"

"That he changed his mind. Is that it, Georgiana?" he questioned. "Did you mean to spend this morning with Fitzwilliam, not simply joining us for breakfast?"

She shrugged her response, continuing not to meet his steady gaze. "The colonel has been from home for so long. I wanted him to know how very much we have missed his presence at Pemberley."

Darcy was not so certain his sister spoke the whole truth; yet, he did not chastise her. Instead, he said, "Let us take our conversation and ourselves to the morning room. Since you are up so early, there is no reason for you to return to your quarters." He walked her slowly down the stairs, while organizing his thoughts on what he would say to her. Inside the room, he seated her at the table on his right before asking, "Might I fill you a plate? I may be a poor substitute, in your mind, for my cousin, but, nevertheless, I would enjoy your company as I claim more coffee and some of Cook's porridge. She always adds a bit of honey, making it tastier."

"That would be pleasant," she said, and Darcy motioned Mr. Nathan to pour tea for his sister and coffee for him.

As he filled her plate with her favorites, he heard Miss Bennet's voice say, *"Miss Darcy's pining for the colonel's attentions."* Last evening, Darcy had thought Miss Bennet's assumption faulty. Now, he was not so self-assured.

He set a plate before her and sat at his usual place along the table. "It is my understanding that you and your friends mean to go into the village today. Is that correct?"

"Yes," she said after chewing her eggs. "Such is the reason I wanted to spend time with Edward before we separated for the better part of the day."

For the moment, Darcy accepted her comment for what it was; yet, doubt had found a place in his mind. "Will it just be you, Miss Whalen and Miss Davidson?"

Georgiana frowned. "I believe Miss Bingley and Mrs. Hurst will also travel into the village in Mr. Hurst's carriage, although, when last I spoke to her, Miss Bingley's plans were not as well-defined as mine."

"What of the countess and Miss Bennet?" he asked in what he hoped sounded of casualness.

Georgiana's nose scrunched up in disapproval. "The countess is not likely to rise until noon, and Miss Whalen, Miss Davidson, and I do not require a chaperone."

"And Miss Bennet? The lady is comparable in age to Miss Bingley," he said innocently.

"She is a governess, William," she argued.

Darcy motioned Mr. Nathan from the room before speaking. "Miss Bennet is a guest in our house, Georgiana, and should be provided the opportunity to join in the activities," he reprimanded.

"You cannot mean to foist the woman on me," she argued.

"When did my sweet sister become a harridan?" he countered. "You cannot think to win the colonel's affirmation if you present Miss Bennet a direct cut."

"Surely, you must comprehend an arrangement with Miss Bennet is not for our cousin's benefit," she contested. "You must speak sense to him."

"I will do no such thing," Darcy declared. "Fitzwilliam would no more appreciate my interference in his life than I would his in mine." He should have bitten back the next retort, but he said, "I recall a girl of fifteen who did not appreciate being told what to do. How do you think a man of five and thirty will respond?"

She flinched at his reprimand, but she did not look away, which was a telling point to how much she had grown into womanhood, although she had not yet learned diplomacy. "I was foolish then, but I have since learned my lessons." Darcy thought she

REGINA JEFFERS

could use a few more. "If you refuse to speak to the colonel, then the conversation falls to me."

Darcy leveled a steady gaze upon her. "I guarantee your doing so will only anger Fitzwilliam. Think upon it, Georgiana. You were angry with my ill-timed words at Ramsgate. What do you expect a man of the world will think of your interference in his life? I would suggest instead of a confrontation with the colonel, who would likely up and leave Pemberley, perhaps forever, that you make a genuine attempt to discover something in Miss Bennet to admire."

"Is that what you are doing? I saw how you watched her closely last evening," she said sarcastically.

"The countess and I are attempting to learn more of the woman." He reached out to caress the back of his sister's hand, holding it tighter when she made to pull it free. "Georgiana, I spoke to Fitzwilliam, as has our aunt. The colonel assures both the countess and me that he and Miss Bennet hold an understanding. We both know our cousin would never walk away from anyone to whom he has presented his promise. Fitzwilliam holds too much honor to act in disgrace."

"Is there any chance Miss Bennet will withdraw?" she asked softly.

He knew his words would dash Georgiana's hopes, but Darcy said them, nonetheless. "A woman in dire circumstances would be a fool to step away from such a grand gesture, and, from what little I know of Miss Bennet, although I suspect the lady dearly loves a bit of laughter in her life, the lady is not foolish."

"Then Edward is lost to us?" she said sadly.

"Soon there will be another branch on the Fitzwilliam family tree," he observed. "As to your statement, the colonel will never be lost to us. An addition will occur. The lady will soon be your cousin, Georgiana. For Fitzwilliam's sake, learn to adore her as I am certain she will adore you."

"Do you 'adore' her?" she asked in crisp tones.

Darcy fought the urge to blush. His thoughts concerning Miss Bennet were as futile as were his sister's regarding their cousin. "Our acquaintance is short-lived, but, beyond her apparent poverty and a tendency to speak her opinion more freely than do most women," he

56

chuckled to permit his sister to know he teased, rather than to criticize, "I find the lady delightful."

* * *

Elizabeth discovered Miss Darcy in the library. "Good day, Miss Darcy," she greeted the girl with a proper curtsey. "May I have a moment of your time?"

The girl frowned, but she nodded her acceptance.

Over the last five years, Elizabeth had learned several hard lessons regarding her place in society, and, so, she dropped her eyes in submission, when, in reality, she and the girl were equals: both daughters of the landed gentry. "Mrs. Reynolds mentioned that you were to travel into the village this morning with your friends."

"And you wish to join us?" the girl asked in obvious disdain, which Elizabeth understood, although she did not appreciate the girl's venom any more than she had appreciated Lady Newland's. "I would not expect you to be so bold as to ask to be—"

The girl stopped in mid-sentence, but Elizabeth perfectly comprehended the girl's disapproval. "To be included in your party? No, Miss Darcy, I would not be so brazen as to ask a favor where none had been extended. I am very well aware of my present place in society."

The girl blushed thoroughly, but she did not retreat. Although she was the object of the young lady's scorn, Elizabeth still respected Miss Darcy for speaking openly. "Are you?" the girl accused. "I wonder."

Elizabeth sighed heavily and curtseyed a second time. "I fully discern your disdain, Miss Darcy. It grieves me greatly that I have offended you by speaking to you without being spoken to first. I did not mean to impose on you for myself, but rather for my maid, who wished the opportunity to spend some time with her family in Lambton. As it is so bitterly cold, I thought it would be a treat for Hannah to ride into the village with your coachman. I thought I might provide her a little longer with her family than if she had to walk, but it was improper of me to think to give pleasure to a mere maid. Pardon my offense, which was not executed intentionally." She turned to leave.

"Wait!" Miss Darcy called. "You asked for a favor for your maid?"

"It was of no consequence, Miss Darcy," she said with an abbreviated curtsey.

"Who is the girl's family?" Miss Darcy demanded.

"Mr. Crownley," Elizabeth responded.

Miss Darcy nodded her understanding, but made no apologies. "Tell the maid we plan to leave at half past ten of the clock."

Elizabeth swallowed the retort rushing to her lips. Instead, she curtseyed once again. "Your kindness will be very welcomed, Miss Darcy, by both my maid and me. I thank you graciously."

Leaving the girl behind, she headed toward the main staircase, not daring to venture too far from the passageways she had learned. Elizabeth suspected if she ventured too far from the prescribed paths, she might become lost forever, not that being lost in such a grand house as Pemberley would be a hardship, but, obviously, forgetting her place in life again would be. She had erroneously thought that a girl raised by a man such as Mr. Darcy would possess the same type of generosity of spirit as did he. She found herself sadly mistaken.

As to Pemberley itself, naturally, her experience in grand houses was limited to the few she had viewed with her Aunt and Uncle Gardiner during a visit to the Lake Country a half-dozen years removed, but Elizabeth doubted few in England could compete with Pemberley House, beyond the royal palaces.

Entering the main hall to access the stairs, she encountered a woman sitting alone in the corner and sobbing. Elizabeth glanced around for one of Mr. Darcy's servants to assist the woman, but, finding none, she sat beside the stranger and slipped a handkerchief into the woman's hands.

Despite the cloth being her one handkerchief, the last one she had taken from Longbourn bearing her father's monogram, she shook off the woman's words of refusal. "My father would wish that I share it with you," she said softly. "Mr. Bennet would approve of my doing so."

"But—" the woman began to protest. However, she quickly fell silent when Elizabeth reclaimed the handkerchief to dab away the woman's tears.

"Why do you not tell me your name? I am Miss Bennet, and I am a guest at Pemberley."

"Mrs. Henry, ma'am," the woman said in halting syllables. "I be one of Mr. Darcy's tenants."

Elizabeth smiled at the woman. "When my father was still alive, I would often tend to the issues the tenants brought before him. Would it be of assistance for you to practice your plea to Mr. Darcy with me first? I assume the gentleman is hearing complaints today. Is that correct?"

"I ain't got no complaints, miss," the woman said quickly. "Mr. Darcy be a kind and 'onorable man."

"Then why are you hesitant to speak to him? I recognize the fact Mr. Darcy presents an imposing figure, but . . ."

Mrs. Henry giggled, transforming her face into one of kindness. "The master be a bit starchy." The woman clapped a hand over her mouth and giggled a second time. "But he be as I say, miss, a most 'onorable and fair man."

"Then there is no reason for your tears," Elizabeth summarized. "Mr. Darcy will treat your problem with the type of tenderness he has displayed in the past."

"Mrs. Henry?" a very male voice said from a place off Elizabeth's left shoulder.

She stood immediately to face the master of the house, an apparent half scowl displayed upon his features. "I apologize, Mr. Darcy. Mrs. Henry was feeling quite distraught—" Elizabeth silenced her explanation when the scowl deepened.

Mr. Darcy stepped around Elizabeth to kneel before Mrs. Henry, who Elizabeth realized was struggling to stand. He eased the woman back down. "Come now, my dear lady," he said in soft tones. "There is no reason for tears."

"But me dearest Mr. Henry be gone," she protested with a return of her tears and sobs. "I've four babes to feed and no man to work the land." Her words were swallowed up by another round of sorrow.

"We will think of something," Mr. Darcy assured.

"But ye require the cottage fer a family who farms the land," Mrs. Henry protested.

Elizabeth sat once again to rest one of her hands upon Mrs. Henry's knee to provide a bit of comfort. "Would it be too presumptuous of me to offer an opinion, Mr. Darcy?" she asked in uncertain tones.

He glanced to her. "If your words have the ability to set about a ready solution, I would welcome your insights, Miss Bennet."

Elizabeth remained uncertain whether he was simply placating her or whether Mr. Darcy was sincere; nevertheless, she rolled her shoulders into place and spoke her piece. "My late father had a similar situation in Hertfordshire. Mr. Bennet placed a young man, who had applied to be tenant at a time when no farms were available, in the home with Mr. Kane's widow."

Mrs. Henry caught at Mr. Darcy's hand. "Be somethin' similar possible, Master?"

Mr. Darcy nodded his gratitude to Elizabeth. "Naturally, I must examine this suggestion from Miss Bennet with care and consult with the steward, Mr. Stanley, but it does seem possible that another young man might be placed into your household. Mr. Braun's son declared himself capable of seeing to his family's farm after he lost both of his parents from consumption, but I had already promised the home farm to another when it became available," he explained. "Jonas Braun means to soon marry Miss Oakes, which means I would be delivering two mouths to feed to your house."

"They both be welcome," Mrs. Henry rushed to say. "They can have me room and I'll bed down with the children."

Elizabeth looked on as Mr. Darcy patted the back of the woman's hand. "Permit me to speak to the steward and Young Braun. If Mr. Braun agrees, I will make arrangements to add another small room onto your cottage." He lifted the woman's chin. "I imagine that Young Braun and Miss Oakes will one day wish to own their own land, but, hopefully, your Jordan will be of age by then. I want Young Braun to teach Jordan what he knows of the land, and I will expect you to teach Miss Oakes not only how to tend a house properly, but to assist her husband with decisions on the crops and the proper rotation thereof to be used on your portion of Pemberley. The land you are charged with tending is quite different from that which the late Mr. Braun farmed."

"Anythin', sir." Mrs. Henry exclaimed with a smile. "Bless you, Mr. Darcy, and bless you, Miss Bennet. You've given me hope when none be had to purchase."

Mr. Darcy assisted the woman to her feet. "Go home. Hug your children tightly. I will have Mr. Stanley bring Young Braun around after the first of the year and settle things between all involved."

Apparently overjoyed, Mrs. Henry presented Elizabeth with a quick hug and Mr. Darcy with both a toothy grin and quick curtsey before scrambling out the side door and high-stepping her way along the path leading to the woods.

Elizabeth said softly, "I know you did not need to leave the property with Mrs. Henry, but your gesture will earn you extensive loyalty among your cottagers."

"Have I also earned a bit of your loyalty, Miss Bennet?" he asked, his eyes appearing to seek an entirely different question, which Elizabeth knew to be a foolish thought, for their acquaintance was barely a day old.

"The day Mr. Bennet discovered a solution that benefitted his cottagers more than him had me knowing true pride in his being my parent. If you permit it, I would claim my share of pride in taking your acquaintance," she said humbly. "Now, if you will pardon me, I must speak to Hannah and then join Mrs. Anderson in the nursery. I have a war to explain to the Hurst boys."

As she walked away, her stomach full of the butterflies Mr. Darcy's presence caused, Elizabeth admitted, if only to herself, the man was by far the most handsome man she would ever know, even out distancing a certain Mr. Wickham, who once held the title based on his comely appearance and easy manner. Obviously, Mr. Darcy's fine appearance was enhanced by a variety of essentials—essentials that enriched his personality and which Mr. Wickham had never claimed.

* * *

Elizabeth returned to her room and rang for Hannah. As she waited for the maid, she splashed some water on her cheeks to cool them. Mr. Darcy's closeness of a few moments earlier, was one she possessed no wish for others to know.

"You rang, miss?" Hannah asked as she breezed into the room, full of what Elizabeth had come to recognize as the girl's customary energy.

Elizabeth turned to face Hannah with a smile. "Yes. I have a surprise for you. I spoke to Miss Darcy a bit ago. She and some of the other ladies plan to travel into the village at half past ten of the clock. Miss Darcy has agreed to your riding on top of the carriage with her coachman. I wish you to go to Lambton and not return until the day after tomorrow."

"What will you do for a dresser?" Hannah protested.

"I am quite capable of dressing myself," Elizabeth countered. She grinned mischievously at the maid. "And if I require someone to dress my hair, I am certain Miss Bingley would be willing to assist me."

"Oh, that one!" Hannah declared with a marked frown upon her countenance. "Those below despise her!"

"Hannah," Elizabeth chastised. "Surely you have misunderstood. Miss Bingley is Mr. Darcy's guest, and I seriously doubt the gentleman would invite people into his home if they would be a burden on his staff."

Hannah shook her head in the negative. "Invited herself, she did. Her and her sister and the lump of a gent the older woman calls a husband. Ride in on their brother's coat tails, they did. Mr. Darcy supposing not to be happy with the gall of the trio. Miss Bingley be thinkin' she is goin' to be the new Mrs. Darcy, but the master be likely to lose, at least, half of his servants if'n he speaks an offer to the woman. Accordin' to Cook, the lady be hangin' on to her hopes before Mr. Darcy married his cousin, Miss Anne. Miss Bingley be desperate. Been nigh onto three years since the master speak his proposal to another, and the lady not be gettin' any younger. I hears tell Mr. Darcy has ordered his valet to sleep in the dressin' room to keep the woman from slippin' inside and claiming herself compromised."

"Oh, my!" Elizabeth said with a giggle. She had desperately missed the days when she and her sisters would gossip together. "What tangled webs we weave!"

"Pardon, miss?" Hannah questioned.

"Just a reference to a Shakespeare play," Elizabeth murmured.

"You be so learned," Hannah remarked. "I wish you be stayin' at Pemberley—that we both be stayin'. I be thinkin' I could have you teach me my letters and sums."

"That would be heavenly," Elizabeth said with a sigh of regret. "I pray Mr. Darcy extends employment to you so you may remain closer to your family, but, as for me, when this short holiday is over, I shall be returning to my world—one where I shall spend the remainder of my days tending some other woman's children."

Chapter seven

"Permit me to assist you," Colonel Fitzwilliam said as Elizabeth juggled a stack of books, which Mr. Darcy had set aside for her use with Mr. Hurst's boys. The colonel claimed half the stack and handed them off to Captain Stewart, who Elizabeth had not known was there because the books had blocked her view. She smiled at the captain in an expression of her gratitude, as the colonel scooped the remainder of the books from her hands.

"What is all this?" the gentleman asked with a lift of his lips in apparent amusement.

"I promised Mr. Hurst's sons that we would reenact battles from our most recent war. Mr. Darcy was kind enough to choose several books from his library that I might use for the lessons."

Again, Colonel Fitzwilliam surveyed the titles, his eyebrow hitching higher. "I do not recall any battles taking place in Derbyshire or the Lake Country."

Elizabeth blushed profusely. "Your cousin also provided me permission to choose something to read from his library for my personal use. As I have previously visited the Lake Country, I thought to refresh my memory, and, as I am currently visiting in Derbyshire, it seemed only appropriate that I should learn something of my surroundings." In reality, she had hoped for a glimmer of information that she might include in a newsy letter to her aunt and her sisters.

"Darcy loves his books nearly as dearly as he loves Pemberley," the colonel remarked with his customary easiness.

"And rightly so," Elizabeth stated. "Both are excessively grand. Your cousin has a right to be proud of the legacy he has created."

The colonel eyed her with what appeared to be skepticism. "Many consider Darcy's pride one of his greatest faults," he observed.

"I have not encountered unruly pride present in Mr. Darcy's nature. Both the gentleman and your mother have been all you said of them and more. They have been excessively kind to me."

The colonel accepted her praise with a nod of his head. "I told you it would be so, did I not?"

"You did, sir."

The colonel looked to his captain. "What say you, Stewart, if we again assist Miss Bennet?" He glanced to her and smiled, which, most assuredly, softened his features; yet, Elizabeth would not compare the colonel to his cousin, who was, in her opinion, superior in many ways, including appearance. "We could provide Hurst's brats with a lesson they will never forget."

"No nightmares, Colonel," Elizabeth protested. "I would not wish to be called before Mr. Darcy to explain myself."

The colonel chuckled easily. "I would not subject you to Darcy's wrath, but I do not want to glorify war: People should know the extent of the devastation it brings so, perhaps they will think twice before sending good men to an early death."

Elizabeth no longer thought the colonel's idea to assist her was a good one, but she was not in a position to criticize his choices. However, when a door opened, and Miss Darcy and her friends stepped into the passageway, a new idea arrived. The ladies had returned from the village earlier than expected. Elizabeth was thankful she had told Hannah not to return until tomorrow, otherwise, the maid would have had little time to share with her family.

"Miss Darcy," she said in a hurry, attempting to ignore the girl's earlier disdain. "How pleasant to encounter you," she rushed to say. "The colonel and Captain Stewart have agreed to aid me in entertaining Mr. Hurst's sons. Would you care to join us? I am certain the colonel would enjoy your presence, would you not, sir?"

The gentleman eyed Elizabeth suspiciously, but he said, "I am certain you would not find my rendition of the Battle of Salamanca entertaining, Georgiana."

The girl shook off the protest. "Nonsense," she declared. "I have no doubt that any story that entertains Miss Bennet will be an equal delight for me. What say you, ladies? Should we accompany my cousin and Captain Stewart to the school room?"

Miss Whalen and Miss Davidson did not appear as enthusiastic as was Miss Darcy, but they nodded their agreement. The colonel extended his arm to Elizabeth. "Are you prepared, my dear?" he asked.

Instead of accepting his arm, Elizabeth scooted around him to claim the two books on local history from the stack the colonel carried. "I shall drop these off in my quarters and follow swiftly," she instructed. "I shall be no more than a minute behind you."

The colonel presented her an odd look, but did as Elizabeth had suggested. "Come along, Georgie." He walked away with Miss Darcy on his arm with the girl looking up at her cousin adoringly. They were followed by Captain Stewart, who was flanked on either side by the other two ladies. "It is as I expected," Elizabeth whispered to their retreating forms. "Mr. Darcy may be blind to Miss Darcy's preference for the colonel, but I am not."

* * *

Finding no one about, Darcy had asked after his cousin only to learn that Fitzwilliam was in the school room with Miss Bennet.

Darcy knew he frowned, but he could not quite quash the idea his cousin and the lady might be enjoying some privacy, while settling things between them. His heart sighed in continued disappointment, but he managed to say, "I will not interrupt them, for now. Where might I find the countess?"

Mr. Nathan also frowned, but, obviously, for a different reason. "I beg your pardon, sir. From what I understand, most of your houseguests are in the nursery. That is, all except Mr. and Mrs. Hurst and Miss Bingley."

Darcy heard his butler's unspoken criticism: *All except those who should be there.* "And what is so fascinating about Pemberley's nursery?" Darcy asked with a lift of his eyebrows.

"I believe Miss Bennet, sir, convinced Colonel Fitzwilliam and Captain Stewart to reenact several of the battles to which they personally stood witness. Initially, Miss Darcy and the other young ladies accompanied the colonel, but I have learned from Mrs. Reynolds that Mr. Bingley and the other two gentlemen soon followed, as did Lady Matlock."

Darcy's lips twitched in amusement. Apparently, Mr. Nathan did not know whether to approve of this turn of events or not. "As I possess a legitimate excuse to call upon the nursery, I believe I will follow the others."

"As is reasonable," Mr. Nathan said as he bowed.

Darcy smiled. "If the party is interrupting Cassandra's nap, I will be sending them down for tea. You might warn Cook."

"Immediately, sir."

With anticipation, Darcy quickly climbed the steps to the nursery. He paused briefly at the door to survey the room. The colonel and Captain Stewart were describing the evening of the Duchess of Richmond's ball in Brussels. As if they had rehearsed it, the young gentlemen in the room claimed the hand of one of the ladies, including Mrs. Anderson, and began to waltz their partners about in small circles, for the room was too cramped to move about freely. Even Hursts' sons danced around with Megs.

It was only then that he realized the gentlemen ignored Miss Bennet's presence in the room. The lady was framed by the window, and she was dancing, only Miss Bennet was dancing with his young daughter. Without considering his actions, Darcy slipped into the room and was standing before her when she turned around. A large smile, likely intended for his daughter or the exercise graced her lips, but he did not hesitate: Darcy placed both the woman and his child in a loose embrace and turned them in a slow circle. "Good afternoon, pumpkin," he said as he bent his head to kiss the top of his daughter's head, but his eyes never left Miss Bennet's shocked gaze.

"Mr. Darcy," she began in apology, attempting to step from his arms, but he tightened his hold just enough to dissuade her. As the rest of the room hummed the music, Darcy said softly, "I am dancing with my daughter and the most—"

However, at that moment, Colonel Fitzwilliam called out. "That is the moment when Wellington received the message of Bonaparte's advance. We departed the ball, many of us still wearing our evening shoes and trousers. Partners were left upon the dance floor, some women receiving a brief kiss in parting." Although Darcy had yet to move, he knew from the sound of giggles behind him, many women in the room received a chaste kiss on their foreheads or their hands.

Such was not what Darcy wished to kiss: Miss Bennet's lips were so tempting, for the briefest of seconds, the rest of those within the room disappeared.

Then a laughing Mrs. Anderson appeared at his side to reach for Darcy's daughter. "It'll be impossible to convince Miss Cassandra to sleep now that she has waltzed with her father. Even so, permit me to take her, Miss Bennet."

Darcy reluctantly released his hold on Miss Bennet and his daughter. He scooped the child from Miss Bennet's hold and lifted Cassandra into the air, teasing another giggle from his daughter's lips before he deposited her into Mrs. Anderson's waiting arms.

He knew Miss Bennet took several steps backward, retreating to the window, just as he turned to the rest of the room.

"Darcy!" his cousin called. "When did you join us?"

"Only a few moments ago," he said with a well-placed smile. "I came to inform each of you that I ordered tea to be delivered to the blue sitting room. However, I did not wish to disturb your tale or the effects of the duchess's ball on everyone." He glanced to Cassandra. "I stole a moment to dance with my daughter and enjoy her smile."

Bingley said, "I thought Miss Bennet entertained Miss Cassandra."

With difficulty, Darcy kept the scowl from his features, along with the desire to slap his friend across the back of Bingley's head. He could not understand why none of the gentlemen in the room would think to partner Miss Bennet. If Mrs. Anderson and Megs deserved partners, why did not a gentleman's daughter—a woman with impeccable manners and a delightful personality. Moreover, if Miss Bennet was Fitzwilliam's betrothed, why was his cousin dancing with Georgiana? Obviously, the reason the colonel had agreed to this venture was to please Miss Bennet. "She did," Darcy said with more calm than he felt. "I imposed on the lady to hold Cassandra while Miss Bennet and I took a few turns together.

Cassandra did not appear to want to leave the good lady's care, even to dance with her father."

Georgiana lifted her chin in a gesture Darcy had never viewed her using previously and one of which he did not approve. It was very reminiscent of a gesture Miss Bingley often employed when criticizing others. "The tea will become cold; therefore, we should go below. I, for one, have had enough of the war for one day. Countess, might you lead?"

Darcy noted the countess's dismay. "Will you join us, Darcy?"

"I will follow in a few minutes. I wish to spend a bit of time with Cassandra before she falls asleep," he said in encouragement.

The group nodded their acceptance and departed two-by-two, leaving only the boys, Megs, Mrs. Anderson, Cassandra, and Miss Bennet behind.

Darcy waited until the sound of their voices died away before he turned to Miss Bennet. "Will you not join us, ma'am?"

"I think not," she said softly. "I believe I will rest for a bit, that is, if Mrs. Anderson and Megs can oversee the nursery."

"You are not employed by Pemberley," he reminded her. "You are a guest."

"I prefer to be of use to the household," she argued.

"It is not necessary," he corrected, "but I shan't chastise you."

With a quick nod of farewell, the lady made her exit. Darcy again reached for his daughter. "Were you having a good time with Miss Bennet?" he asked as he settled his child in his arms. Cassandra patted his cheeks in that adorable way of all small children.

"Miss Bennet has a way with both Miss Cassandra and Mr. Hurst's sons," Mrs. Anderson declared. "It be a shame she be in her situation, for she'd make some man a good wife and a mother for his children."

Darcy agreed, but he would not be that man, and that particular idea displeased him more than he would ever admit to another. He stifled a groan of despair when he realized that when Colonel Fitzwilliam married Miss Bennet, they would often be in company together. He did not know whether he could tolerate the situation or not. Of course, if Fitzwilliam married, his cousin would likely move into the estate that would be his inheritance, which was located in Oxfordshire. Perhaps distance would provide Darcy time to control his jealousy.

After playing with Cassandra for a quarter hour, Darcy turned his steps toward where his guests were congregated, but as he crossed the passageway leading past Miss Bennet's quarters, he stopped to consider what must be a strong case of insanity. Had the gentlemen ignored the lady because of her dowdy attire? Had they not noticed her splendid personality because it was hidden behind the "dull curtain" she presented for all to look upon? What would be the result if she made an appearance in something more appropriate? Without taking a full account of the consequences, he paused outside her door and knocked.

Within seconds, the lady opened the door. "Mr. Darcy? Is something amiss, sir?"

For the briefest of moments, he thought to push past her and spend time alone with her in her room, but, instead, he assured, "Nothing unusual. It simply occurred to me that perhaps you might feel from place when we gather." He paused in awkwardness. Without a doubt, he should have thought over his actions before knocking. "I assure you, ma'am, I do not wish to sound condescending, but I thought you might have use of a few of my late wife's gowns. You are shorter than was Anne," he rushed to say, "and . . ." He glanced to her figure and willed the blush away. "If you are handy with a needle, I am certain you could find a use for several of the dresses."

"I could not think to impose—" she began her protest.

"The gowns will be presented to a rag man when he calls upon the estate after the new year begins," he declared. "Surely you could find a better use for any number of them. The late Mrs. Darcy was quite modest; therefore, the newer ones should serve you well. You would have new things for your new life." The idea of her wearing something he had provided her pleased him. Even if she was to marry Fitzwilliam, she would think of him when she wore the gowns. It was the best he could do for now.

"I do not know what to say, Mr. Darcy. You have already been more than kind to me," she declared.

"Nonsense," he insisted. "I will ask Mrs. Reynolds to choose several among Anne's gowns and assist you with your fittings."

The woman reached out to catch his hand. Wrapping her two smaller ones around his, she said with tears misting her eyes, "When the colonel suggested that I join him at Pemberley, I did not believe anyone would be as open in his welcome as you have proven to be. Your generosity has renewed my soul." She brought the back of his hand to her lips to plant a gentle kiss on it. Heat raced up Darcy's arm, and his breath caught in his chest. Yet, before he could react, she stepped back. "No one would ever believe my good fortune in taking Colonel Fitzwilliam's acquaintance. Bless you, sir." With that, the lady closed the door to her quarters, leaving Darcy in the empty passageway and wanting more.

* * *

Elizabeth had not gone below for supper, sending word that she would take Mrs. Anderson's place in the nursery long enough for the older woman to spend an evening with her daughter's family in Lambton. It was there that Mrs. Reynolds found her.

"Good evening, Miss Bennet."

"Good evening, Mrs. Reynolds. Is there something I may do to assist you?"

Mrs. Reynolds glanced to the sleeping children. "You have a magical way about you when it comes to children. You remind me very much of the master's mother, Lady Anne Darcy. The late mistress adored Master William and had wanted more children. Pemberley grieved when she lost two little ones before Miss Georgiana came along. Unfortunately, her health and her spirit suffered from the multiple disappointments. Yet, when she was alive, the children in the neighborhood all came to Pemberley, as much for her as they did to spend time with Master William."

Elizabeth admitted, "There was a time when I never considered the possible pleasure of tending to a child, of being an observer of each of the measures of their growth, and playing a part in steadying their walk into adulthood." She smiled sadly. "Now that I fully understand both the responsibility and the reward of playing this most important role in life, I am faced with the reality of never claiming children of my own."

Mrs. Reynolds said sagely, "Perhaps God simply wanted you to learn a valuable lesson before he presented you with another opportunity."

Elizabeth shook off the idea. "I am simply thankful for all the memories I have sowed here at Pemberley. They shall sustain me over the remainder of my days. It was most providential to take Colonel Fitzwilliam's acquaintance and to be presented the pleasure of knowing the colonel's family. Pemberley and its master are incomparable, in my humble opinion."

Mrs. Reynolds's expression was an odd one, but she said, "Megs will remain with the children until Mrs. Anderson returns. If you are not too exhausted by your day, I thought we might have a look at the gowns Mr. Darcy promised you."

Elizabeth blushed thoroughly. "It was exceedingly kind of Mr. Darcy to make the offer, but I would not wish for the gentleman to look upon a gown and see his late wife's clothes upon another woman. I would not wish to bring more sorrow to his door.'"

Mrs. Reynolds frowned deeply. "I should not say this, for the master would not approved; however, the wedding between Mr. Darcy and his cousin, Miss Anne, was not a love match. It was an arrangement to satisfy his aunt."

"Lady Matlock?" Elizabeth asked.

"No, his mother's sister, who was the eldest of the three Fitzwilliam children and who always claimed an arrangement had existed between herself and Lady Anne Darcy for a match between Mr. Darcy and Miss Anne since the time they were in the nursery, as are these children right now."

"I see, Elizabeth said softly.

"I should not have spoken from turn," Mrs. Reynolds said in self-chastisement, while a blush marked the woman's still smooth cheeks. "What I meant to say was Mr. Darcy be not the type of man to know one gown from the next. His eyes glaze over when women speak of fripperies and cloth and such. He would not have even thought of the dresses if I had not inquired of his preference for their disposition last week. In truth, he has never been faced with making such a decision or even considered what must be done after a woman's death. He thoroughly understood what was required by his

73

father's passing, but, since Lady Anne Darcy died when he was just twelve, the master would be slow to think on such responsibility."

Elizabeth nodded her acceptance of the woman's words, before gesturing to her well-worn day dress. "Surely the gowns are of better quality than the one I currently wear."

Mrs. Reynolds smiled easily. "Most assuredly the master will realize the difference, but the others will not. I certainly shall not speak of Mr. Darcy's generosity to the rest of those gathered at Pemberley. In fact, I was thinking, perhaps a small trunk had arrived for you, sent forward by—"

"Lady Newland," Elizabeth supplied.

"A trunk for you arrived from Lady Newland with the remainder of your belongings—a few simple gowns and accessories. It would seem to me that even a governess would sometimes be called upon to dine with the family and their guests. No one else must know the truth."

Elizabeth could not believe such a fine woman would go to the lengths Mrs. Reynolds was suggesting to protect her. It had been so long since anyone gave a care to her welfare. The idea sent tears rushing to her eyes. "God has blessed me by bringing me to Pemberley, ma'am. It is truly a magical place."

Mrs. Reynold smiled largely. "I have been telling others exactly that for more years than I care to recall. Now, come along. I chose three gowns that will go well with your hair and complexion. These will all require a hem and perhaps a line of lace, which I have in the bag I am carrying, but I am certain you will adore each."

Chapter eight

Tuesday, 22 December 1818

Darcy should have been clearing his desk of correspondence so he might spend time with his guests, but he found himself staring out his window, watching as a light dusting of snow covered the ground. If it continued as such, they would see their first measurable snow of the season. It would be necessary for him to organize activities to keep his guests entertained inside if things turned worse. The men, for example, would not be able to go shooting again until the snowfall ceased.

A light knock at the door announced Lady Matlock's presence. "Might you spare me a few minutes?"

Darcy turned to face her. A weak smile turned up the corners of his mouth. "I should have known you would be as troubled by yesterday's events as am I."

"I have pondered over it all evening and most of the night, but I have no explanation for this odd arrangement between my son and Miss Bennet on this day any more than I did when the pair stepped down before Pemberley two days prior."

Darcy smiled easily. Lady Matlock was as intense as he where family was involved. "Would you prefer a small sherry or should I send for tea?"

She shook her head in dismay. "I should have the tea, for it is still early in the day, but I shall have the sherry."

As Darcy poured them both a drink, his aunt seated herself before the fire. At length, handing her the drink, he sat heavily beside her. "I will permit you to begin. How came you to be in the nursery with the others?"

Her ladyship took a small sip of the sherry before she spoke. "Actually, it was my lady's maid who told me of the gathering. Margaret said Miss Bennet had convinced Fitzwilliam and Captain Stewart to aid her in telling Mr. Hurst's sons about the war." She paused to sigh heavily. "At first, I was concerned, fearing Miss Bennet had asked the impossible for my son. You and I have spoken previously of my concerns regarding what the war has done to my youngest boy's good nature. Edward puts on a fine face for the world, but someday soon his soul will ask for an accounting of his actions. I was prepared to rush to the nursery to oversee the activities, but, then, Margaret told me Miss Bennet had also asked Georgiana and my niece's friends to join them. As I set out for the nursery, I also learned Mr. Bingley and the two local gentlemen had followed the ladies."

"I was on my way to spend time with Cassandra," Darcy explained, "when I learned that the majority of my houseguests, except the Hursts and Miss Bingley, were all in the nursery." Such was partially true: He had meant to call upon Cassandra, but he had been equally enticed by the idea of spending a few minutes with Miss Bennet. Darcy was not proud of his actions, but he could not seem to control himself where that particular lady was concerned. He had attempted to convince himself that he missed an intelligent woman's comfort and conversation; yet, the truth was that Anne had provided him neither.

"I was within," the countess continued, "for perhaps three-quarters of an hour. Never once during that time did Fitzwilliam offer Miss Bennet more than the occasional glance nor did she look upon my son with more than a look of approval as he wove his tale. One would assume if they are betrothed, they would periodically look upon each other with fondness."

"I have experienced like thoughts," Darcy admitted. "Perhaps my cousin and the lady decided they would not share their happiness until after Christmastide—to provide us all time to form an honest opinion of the lady."

"Perhaps," the countess mused aloud. "Although I cannot imagine the reason for their secrecy. Even if we objected, there is little we could do but accept Fitzwilliam's decision. They are both of age."

"Knowing the colonel, I suspect he would wish us to welcome the lady on her merits, not because he had chosen her," Darcy argued.

Lady Matlock sighed again. "Surely my son does not think I would send the woman away. I am not the earl. I know previously you and I have had a good laugh regarding the necessity to find Miss Bennet a more illustrious position, however, in my short acquaintance with the lady, I have found myself growing fond of her. Miss Bennet appears to be both sensible and kind."

Darcy said cautiously, "I would agree. Ignoring her reduced circumstances, Fitzwilliam has discovered a rare rough diamond, who only requires the colonel's tender care in order to shine fully."

"Then we are in agreement?" the countess questioned.

Darcy cleared his throat in discomfort. "All except, mayhap, Georgiana. Have you noticed how my sister has clung to Fitzwilliam and how Georgiana speaks quite rudely to Miss Bennet?"

The countess looked to Darcy with new eyes. "Do you think our Georgiana has developed feelings for Fitzwilliam?"

"Miss Bennet seemed to think so. If you recall, the lady spoke to the nature of Georgiana and Edward's connection that first evening we were all together," he attested.

Her ladyship frowned. "Do you think Fitzwilliam is aware of this turn of events?"

"Not that I have noted, but I will, most assuredly, be more observant. Moreover, I feel an obligation to speak to my sister regarding her recent behavior. It is unconscionable for her to be rude to a guest in this house. Our parents would highly disapprove."

"As my son has spoken his own 'obligation' to Miss Bennet, it is foolish for Georgiana to think she might change Fitzwilliam's mind. The colonel is a man of honor. Even if Georgiana proved to be Edward's choice, which I am not yet convinced such is so, nothing can be done if Miss Bennet wishes to claim the colonel's offer of his hand."

"And here I thought Christmastide at Pemberley would be a simple matter for all to enjoy."

* * *

"Miss Bennet, what have you there?" Hannah asked when she spotted the dark green day dress to which Elizabeth had spent a good portion of last evening and this morning making adjustments. The gown had been presented to her by Mrs. Reynolds.

"Is it not lovely?" Elizabeth held the gown to her chest, caressing the fabric with her fingers. "Mrs. Reynolds made me a gift of the gown." She laughed self-consciously. "I am certain my mother would be pleased to repeat her 'I told you so's' regarding my lack of skill with a needle, but I do not care at this moment. In truth, I would quite welcome them just to view her face when I wear this gown. Mrs. Bennet repeatedly chastised me for a variety of what she determined were my 'deficits,' but spending more time tending to my stitches was a favorite of hers," she explained. "You have no idea how many times I have adjusted the side seams of this gown, but it was worth it." She sighed contentedly. "It has been so long since I first felt more than simply 'adequate' in a dress."

Hannah caught up the other two dresses—a red one and a yellow one. "Mrs. Reynolds be presentin' you these also?"

"Mr. Darcy suggested that she do so," Elizabeth admitted. "The dresses belonged to the late Mrs. Darcy."

"And he offered them to you?" Hannah's eyebrow rose in amazement.

"The gentleman did me a great favor," Elizabeth said reverently. "These three had only been worn but a few times. From what Mrs. Reynolds shared, the late Mrs. Darcy was customarily quite thin and frail, and her dresses would, generally, never have fit me. However, these were made to see the lady through her lying in. According to Mr. Darcy's housekeeper, I am shorter and more, how did she say it, more 'buxomy' than the estate's former mistress."

"My father says the village was surprised Mr. Darcy went and married his cousin. My father, Mr. Crownley, called the lady 'pale and sickly.'"

Elizabeth placed a hand on Hannah's arm. "We shall not speak poorly of the lady."

Hannah dropped her eyes. "Yes, miss."

"I am not upset with you," Elizabeth was quick to say. "But as the gentleman has presented me a true kindness, I shall never speak out against him."

"You be correct, miss," Hannah declared with a smile. "Tell me what you wish me to do with these two dresses. I am handy with a needle."

Elizabeth smiled easily on the girl. "I am blessed by Mr. Darcy's generosity and yours." She reached for the red gown. "Permit me to show you where adjustments are required by slipping this on. Meanwhile, tell me all about your visit with your family. Were they surprised to have you at home sooner than they expected?"

As the girl pinned the seams and the hem, Elizabeth listened contentedly to Hannah's animated tale. Secretly, she wished for just one day to spend with her mother. Even if Mrs. Bennet chastised her the whole time, Elizabeth would be humble and happy.

* * *

"Miss Bennet," Mr. Nathan said as Elizabeth made to enter the drawing room where the guests were to gather before supper.

She turned to the butler. "Yes, sir. May I be of assistance?"

The man smiled upon her. "Only a moment of your time, miss. Mrs. Henry called about an hour earlier, asking for you. I told her she must wait until you came down."

Elizabeth glanced about the foyer for Mrs. Henry. "Is the woman still here?"

"In the morning room, miss. I presented her a cup of tea and asked her to wait for you there."

Elizabeth's anxiousness faded. "I should have known you would handle the situation appropriately, sir. Thank you for showing Mrs. Henry a kindness." She turned toward the room on her left, and Mr. Nathan scrambled to reach it before her.

"I will announce you, miss," he said in that no-nonsense way of all upper servants.

Elizabeth reached out to the man and patted his arm. "I am no great lady, sir. There is no reason to announce me."

Mr. Nathan shook off her words. "Each of us, miss, knows our place in the household. I understand you consider yourself a governess, an occupation that is neither servant nor mistress in the hierarchy of a great house. However, at Pemberley, Mr. Darcy named you as one of his honored guests, and I will treat you as such."

Elizabeth studied the man's expression closely. "I do apologize, Mr. Nathan," she said, at last, "if my actions have placed you in an awkward position. It was not intentionally done. When I was still in my father's house, I fear Mr. Bennet provided me much latitude in my decisions, but I promise you I can and will perform as the lady Mr. Darcy expects me to be." She smiled mischievously. "That is, assuming you hold no objection to my spending some of my time on the floor of Pemberley's nursery with Miss Cassandra."

"As you well know, miss," the man said as a small smile turned up the corners of his lips, "I would approve of anyone who displayed kindness to Mr. Darcy's daughter." With that, he opened the door to the morning room to say, "Miss Bennet."

Elizabeth pulled her shoulders back and walked past the man to say, "Mrs. Henry, what an extraordinarily pleasant surprise. How might I be of service, ma'am?"

Mrs. Henry scrambled to her feet to curtsy. "Thank you for seeing me, miss."

"Gladly done, Mrs. Henry."

"I shan't keep you, miss," the woman said with a toothy smile. "I came to bring you this." Mrs. Henry handed Elizabeth a folded over piece of paper.

Elizabeth took it gingerly and carefully opened the flap to expose a small lace doily. "How exquisite," she murmured as she fingered the thread. "But I should not accept this. Surely another deserves this more than I."

"I made it special for you, miss," the woman insisted. "I thought you might use it with the brooch you wear."

Elizabeth touched the pin on her dress. "The brooch belonged to my paternal grandmother and contains a snippet of my father's hair when he was a boy." She looked again to the lace circle. "I would be honored to wear your gift, Mrs. Henry."

Before the woman could respond, Colonel Fitzwilliam appeared in the open doorway. "What have we here, Miss Bennet?"

As Mrs. Henry curtseyed again, Elizabeth explained, "Mrs. Henry brought me a small fairing as a reward for assisting her with a request made of Mr. Darcy."

The colonel appeared confused, but he accepted the small piece of lace in his palm. "Is it not the most delicate piece of lace you have ever seen?" Elizabeth asked.

The colonel touched it with his fingertip. "I would honestly say it rivals some of the lace I viewed in Brussels."

Elizabeth turned to Mrs. Henry. "You made this quite quickly. Do you often make such pieces, ma'am?"

"When I can afford the thread, miss. In fact, there be more than a dozen of Mr. Darcy's tenants who be handy with a needle. A few better than me."

The colonel eyed Elizabeth suspiciously. "I recognize that look, Miss Bennet. That is the same look you sported when you convinced me and Stewart to join you and the children in the nursery yesterday. What idea has taken root in your pretty head?"

Elizabeth easily blushed. "Nothing I can speak of at this moment." She turned to the waiting Mrs. Henry. "I shall cherish your generosity, ma'am, but I should allow you to return home to your children. Moreover, I imagine the others are waiting for the colonel's appearance and mine in the drawing room."

Mr. Nathan said, "I will show you out, Mrs. Henry." Another round of curtsies had the woman following Mr. Nathan through a servant door.

"Shall we?" the colonel asked, offering Elizabeth his arm.

She slid her hand about his elbow. "If we are tardy, sir, you must know I shall blame you."

The colonel chuckled. "I would expect nothing less."

A footman opened the door to expose the others gathered within the drawing room. Before she could respond, Colonel Fitzwilliam announced, "You must pardon my lateness. Miss Bennet waylaid me with a piece of lace."

Elizabeth laughed easily, for he had claimed the upper hand. Softly, she said, "You must realize, sir, you have declared war upon my sensibilities, and I do not concede defeat easily."

* * *

Darcy looked up at the sound of Fitzwilliam's voice, but his cousin's presence in the room was not what drew Darcy's attention. It was Miss Bennet's appearance that stole Darcy's breath away. He had previously thought her fetching, but dressed in a simple green gown and with her hair styled, the lady was, by far, at least for him, the most interesting woman in the room. If Anne had been half as beautiful in that same gown, Darcy might have paid his late wife more consideration. Beyond familial affection, he had never loved Anne de Bourgh, and their marriage had been a farce in the making, but, until this instant, he had thought they might have made a go of it. Unfortunately, for both of them, it was not meant to be. Darcy regretted Anne's death, for she was Cassandra's mother, and he held firsthand knowledge of how growing up without a mother could affect a young woman, but he was grateful to be released from the obligation to his late wife. In truth, he sometimes privately wondered if Anne had chosen to leave this earthly world rather than to face a life as his wife.

Fitzwilliam led Miss Bennet to an open settee, seated the woman, and sat beside her. It was a sobering moment for Darcy, for, up to this very moment, he had not viewed his cousin and the lady together, especially, as they were laughing and enjoying an intimate conversation as a couple. Darcy's heart clenched in denial.

"What do you find so amusing, Fitzwilliam?" the countess asked. Darcy noticed that Lady Matlock watched the interaction between her son and Miss Bennet as carefully as did Darcy. However, he was certain the contentment on his aunt's face did not match the scowl forming on his own.

"We are speaking of music and of lace and war, your ladyship," Darcy's cousin said with a large smile of satisfaction.

"Of music?" the countess asked, ignoring her son's cryptic explanation. "Do you play and sing, Miss Bennet? We have yet to hear you display on the instrument."

"A little, ma'am," Miss Bennet assured. "My sister Mary is the most musically-inclined of our family."

"Then some time or other we shall be happy to hear you. The Pemberley instrument is a superior one."

"Did your governess not insist upon your becoming proficient upon, at least, one instrument?" Miss Bingley asked, and Darcy sat taller in preparation to intervene if required. He easily recognized the tone Miss Bingley employed. The lady meant to provide Miss Bennet a set down. What was worse was the fact Georgiana sat beside Bingley's sister and looked on with satisfaction. "You should all have learned something of music."

"We never had a governess," Miss Bennet explained. The woman appeared more amused than offended by Miss Bingley's attitude.

"No governess!" Mrs. Hurst accused in obvious support of her sister. Darcy had always despised their spiteful behavior to others. "How was that possible? You spoke of four sisters. Imagine five sisters brought up at home without a governess. Such does not speak well to your avowed occupation, does it? I never heard of such a thing!"

Darcy's ire rose quickly. How dare Bingley's sisters attack one of his guests! He was half-tempted to order them from the house.

"Your mother must have been a slave to your education," Miss Bingley accused.

"I assure you, ma'am, such was not the case," Miss Bennet responded. How she handled this situation was proving quite odd to Darcy, and, he suspected, to the countess. A smile marked Miss Bennet's lips, and a slight lift of her chin said Miss Bennet was leading Bingley's sisters toward a retort that would readily put an end to their snideness. In truth, he was mesmerized by the efficacy with which Miss Bennet handled the open attack by Caroline Bingley.

Miss Bingley, thinking herself superior, continued. "Then who taught you? Who attended to you? Without a governess you must have been neglected."

Miss Bennet held Caroline Bingley's gaze an elongated moment before responding. "I suppose compared with 'some' families, especially those in London or 'those who wished to join fine society,' I believe, in many ways, we were, as you say, 'neglected,' but such of us as wished to learn never wanted the means to do so. Despite earning my keep as a governess, employing such a person in a household does not guarantee a child will learn what she ought. Nor does some sort of threat or punishment.

"My parents took a different approach. My father kept an extensive library, and we were encouraged to read, and we were exposed to all the masters that were necessary.

"As for me, I have read extensively in the classics, history, and more than a sprinkling of science tomes. I speak French, along with a passable knowledge of German and Italian. In truth, I read both better than I speak the language, but I suppose such is true because many in the rural shires have no use for reading books in other languages. They are simply pleased to read and know their sums so they may conduct business." She glanced to Darcy. "I imagine you would say the same of your tenants and the villagers, but I digress.

"I possess more than a general knowledge of the world, and, although I am not as proficient on the pianoforte as are you, I am not a novice. I admit I certainly have not the talent which some people possess. My fingers do not move over the instrument in the masterly manner in which I have observed, for example, in Miss Darcy's presentation or those of others I have known previously. My playing has not the same force or rapidity as those, and, I admit, I do not produce the same expression so many women do when called upon to perform. It is not that I do not believe my fingers as capable as any other woman's of superior execution. Instead, I have always supposed my failing to be my fault because I would not take the trouble of practicing.

"However, even with my imperfections, I have been employed by three superior families to instruct their daughters in preparation for their being placed at elite schools for young ladies or making their debut into society."

Colonel Fitzwilliam ended the attack and whatever else Miss Bingley dared to disparage. "I would say most gentlemen would prefer a woman who held interests beyond the perfect color of a ribbon on her bonnet or for fripperies, or who only speaks of who has recently proposed to whom. There are too many gentlemen who seek solace in their clubs rather than to spend an evening with their wives. Ask yourself why such is so. I, for one, wish to marry a woman who cannot only serve as my hostess, if and when I choose to entertain, but also one who can keep me ready company on a cold winter night and offer stimulating conversation, while not boring me with insignificant details."

Darcy silently agreed. Unfortunately, the one woman who might prove to be his perfect match currently kept company with Darcy's favorite cousin.

Chapter nine

It had been one of the longest evenings of his life, at least the longest since he had begun to shun invitations to balls and soirées to avoid the society mama's hoping to entrap him as a husband for their daughters, and he had been glad when the time came for him to retreat to his quarters.

As much as he would wish to deny a recent obsession with Miss Bennet, Darcy had attempted not to glare at the easiness with which Fitzwilliam, and even Captain Stewart, had spent much of the evening with Miss Bennet. Even when Georgiana and Miss Davidson took turns entertaining their party with an evening of music, not to be rivaled by several of London's most acclaimed pianists, Darcy had not listened carefully. Instead, he had cursed himself for wanting to view Miss Bennet in a respectable gown. Despite not wishing to admit his lack of judgement, he, too, had found the lady enchanting and excessively handsome. All would have been well if he had been permitted a few moments with her, simply to satisfy his unspoken need to be in her company, but, after supper, Miss Bennet had joined the countess, Fitzwilliam, and Captain Stewart at the card tables, and Darcy had sat in his corner and brooded, purposely placing a smile of welcome on his lips.

Unfortunately, for him, he had not been aware of Miss Bingley moving a chair closer to where he sat until it was too late for him to retreat.

"I could not help but notice your interest in Miss Bennet," Miss Bingley said conspiratorially. "The lady, most assuredly, is lacking in accomplishments. And to think, she dares to brag of her limited upbringing."

Darcy eyed her with contempt when he responded. "I suppose your opinion of 'accomplished' women comes from what your 'governess' deemed necessary. Like you, I have often heard of women being enamored by a variety of gentlemen for their fine countenances, manners, and accomplishments. Often, men are made aware of a woman's skill at painting tables, covering screens, and netting purses. I scarcely know any woman who cannot claim these so-called 'accomplishments.' Rarely have I not heard of a variety of young ladies spoken of for the first time without being informed that they are very accomplished.

"Your estimation of the common extent of accomplishments has too much truth. Woefully, for you, like my cousin, I am of the persuasion that the word is applied to many women who deserve it not, other than by netting a purse or covering a screen, and I am very far from agreeing with you in your estimation of ladies in general, and Miss Bennet in particular. I cannot boast of knowing more than a half dozen, in the whole range of my acquaintance, that are truly accomplished."

"Oh, certainly," Miss Bingley readily agreed, obviously choosing to ignore the warning in his tone. It amazed Darcy how often she heard only what she wanted to hear. "No one can be readily esteemed as accomplished who does not greatly surpass what is usually met with. A woman must have a thorough knowledge of music, singing, drawing, dancing, and the modern languages, to deserve the word; and, besides all this, she must possess a certain something in her air and manner of walking, the tone of her voice, her addresses and expressions, or the word will be but half-deserved."

Choosing to be quite frank once again, he stated in cold tones, "If you expect me to agree with you, Miss Bingley, you will be sadly disappointed. Most certainly, a man in the higher reaches of society would wish his wife to possess a variety of 'accomplishments,' as you describe them; however, as my cousin clearly stated to all who truly wished to hear and understand his words, an accomplished woman must yet add something more substantial in the improvement of her mind by extensive reading and by her willingness to stand beside her husband in whatever the future holds."

Darcy looked on with interest as Miss Bingley flinched as if he had raised his hand to her: He was well aware that Miss Bingley rarely read anything beyond the society notations in the newsprints.

"I see," she said softly. "Then you, too, admire Miss Bennet."

"My opinion of the lady is none of your concern. Let us simply say that Miss Bennet was an 'invited' guest at Pemberley."

"And I am not?" she said with a lift of her chin in defiance.

"My invitation was addressed to Bingley," he said coldly. "It is my deep fondness for your brother that permits you and your sister's family to intrude upon my goodwill. Yet, such does not permit you the latitude to undermine another of my guests." He rarely spoke so harshly to anyone, but he would not permit others to bring harm to Miss Bennet's name. In that manner, he and Fitzwilliam were in total agreement.

"She is a governess!" Miss Bingley protested.

"While Miss Bennet is at Pemberley, I will expect my other guests to treat the lady with the same respect as I do. I shan't be pleased by anything less than your compliance, and I trust this subject will not be brought before me again."

"Mr. Darcy?"

Darcy looked up from the fire in the grate and his thoughts of the evening's truth to discover his valet near the dressing room door. "Yes, Mr. Sheffield."

"I did not wish to disturb you, sir, but Miss Darcy's maid wished me to inform you that your sister, sir, is very distraught. Ruby says you presented her strict orders several years back to inform you immediately if your sister was 'extremely upset,' no matter the cause or the time of day."

Darcy had done so when Georgiana had withdrawn from her usual pleasant self after Darcy had interrupted a planned elopement on the part of his sister and Darcy's long-time nemesis, Mr. George Wickham. He suspected he knew Georgiana's current woes. They were also his. "Thank Ruby for her diligence and assure her I shan't inform Miss Darcy of her concerns."

"Right away, sir."

His valet disappeared into the dressing room. With a sigh of resignation, Darcy rose to straighten his shirt and cravat. Deciding to leave his jacket behind, he reached for the brandy he had poured earlier and downed it. "Liquid courage," he murmured as he grabbed a fresh handkerchief from the drawer, before departing his quarters to seek out his sister.

In less than a minute, he tapped lightly on her door and waited.

From within came the sound of someone moving about the room. "I am well, Ruby, truly I am," his sister called out.

He leaned closer to speak softly against the wood, "It is William."

Within seconds, his sister released the latch and stepped back to permit him to enter. "Did Ruby inform you that I was upset?" she asked through trembling lips.

Darcy purposely crowded the door, forcing Georgiana backward so he could close the door behind him as he gathered his sister into his arms. "I knew this evening's events would bring you distress," he said gently, as he pushed her hair away from her face so he might look on her features. "I have been comforting your tears since you were but a babe in the cradle. Naturally, I would recognize how our cousin's attentions to Miss Bennet would play ill with your sensibilities."

"Oh, William, what am I to do?" she wailed. "I have wasted more than five years waiting for Fitzwilliam to recognize that I am a woman—not a little girl."

He led her to the bed where they both might sit close. "Men are often a bit daft," he confessed. "I have difficulty thinking of you as more than a young girl with braids following me from room to room. Naturally, our cousin could be of the same mind."

"But I have changed everything to draw Edward's notice. My hair. My dresses," she protested.

Darcy silently admitted that he had taken no notice of what his sister named as "changes." He had assumed her style of dress had altered after she began to "fill out," not because Georgiana wished to draw a particular man's attention. What was he to say to such a confession? He chose simply to pat her on the back and to retrieve the handkerchief he had carried with him to stuff into her waiting hands.

"Fitzwilliam proved this evening that I am not now, nor was I ever, his choice of brides," she declared through a series of shoulder-shaking sobs. "I should . . . I should have listened to you."

"The heart is deaf to such warnings," Darcy said lamely. His own heart had taken a blow of disappointment upon viewing the colonel with Miss Bennet on his arm.

"I thought . . ." Georgiana began and paused suddenly. "Why did you present Miss Bennet with one of Anne's gowns? I held a small chance of distracting the colonel until he saw that woman dressed as a lady," she accused. "When Miss Bennet walked around in her mousy governess dresses, I thought our cousin would notice me, but—"

Darcy said softly, "Anne's gowns would have been presented to charity." The excuse sounded weak, even to his ears. He had foolishly wanted to view Miss Bennet as she was meant to be seen. He rushed to say, "Fitzwilliam wished for the countess's approval of the woman, and I thought to aid his efforts. I never meant to bring harm to your head by doing do. In a proper dress, Miss Bennet would no longer be looked upon as a 'deficit' to any who claimed her acquaintance, and I had hoped to ease the way for the colonel's official announcement of their betrothal."

He realized such would be as equally devastating for him as it would be to his sister. The idea, quite readily, shook Darcy to his core. When had he become so thoroughly inclined to adore his cousin's intended? He had known the woman only a matter of days. "It grieves me, Georgiana," he continued, "that my decision brought you pain and doubts of your self-worth," he said honestly.

"I thought," she admitted with a heavy sigh, "that our cousin would deny his promise to Miss Bennet, but this evening has proven me to be a fool. Even I could openly view why Fitzwilliam would choose Miss Bennet. She is definitely not the epitome of an 'accomplished' woman, as Miss Bingley has often extolled one to be, but Miss Bennet is handsome enough to attract a variety of gentlemen and intelligent enough to hold their interest for longer than a few minutes."

Darcy was not best pleased to learn that Miss Bingley had filled Georgiana's head with that particular woman's brand of venom.

He would be glad to be rid of her after this holiday ended, and he would make certain she would never impose on him again. As the countess had insisted, if necessary, and Darcy held no doubts extremes might be required, he would present Miss Bingley a direct cut while society looked on.

Coming back to the issue at hand, he eased Georgiana from his embrace. "I realize what I am about to say will go against your current state of mind."

"Your tone, at this moment, is the one you use when you wish me to learn a lesson," she said with a lift of her brows.

Darcy smiled lovingly upon her. "Being your brother was so much easier when you were a naïve child wanting me to repair your doll's broken leg."

"You think I did not realize you purchased me a new one when you could not fix the older?" she teased.

"Do not destroy all my illusions in one fell swoop, Georgiana," he teasingly cautioned.

She wiped away the tears from her cheeks. "What is your advice, Brother?"

He tweaked her nose in a gesture of affection. "Perhaps you should befriend Miss Bennet. If the lady is to be a part of our family, you will not be able to avoid her completely, and you would injure the colonel if he thought you disapproved. Miss Bennet is five years your senior and has seen the world in which we live from the other side of the servant's door. I fear we will soon be encountering many changes in our way of life, and she might provide you a different perspective. My first impression of the lady is she is genuine, with no guise about her, and, as you said moments ago, Miss Bennet's attraction goes beyond being an 'accomplished' woman by society's standards."

Georgiana looked at him oddly. "Then you truly understand the colonel's attraction to the woman?"

"I do."

* * *

Wednesday, 23 December 1818

Darcy had not recovered from his sleepless night when Lady Matlock discovered him holed up in his study. "Good. You are alone," she announced as she claimed the seat before his desk.

"I am customarily alone in my study," he quipped.

A raised eyebrow said her ladyship questioned his tone without vocalizing her concern. "I thought perhaps the gentlemen were hiding in here with you, but I learned from Mr. Nathan that my son has decided the men should bring out the sleighs. I have been told by your servant that there is enough snow for them to travel easily over the hills, but not so chilly outside that the ladies will become too cold from the air."

"I see," he remarked. "And what is my part in this adventure? Fitzwilliam did not consult me on the use of the sleighs; therefore, I cannot have a say in their fun." He shrugged his supposed "indifference." "Obviously, they have no need for a widower to generate enjoyable entertainments."

His aunt ignored Darcy's woebegone attitude. "Then you do not intend to join the group?"

For a brief second, Darcy considered how pleasant it might be to share a sleigh with Miss Bennet, but he did not think he could bear an afternoon watching his cousin wooing the woman. "I must oversee the preparations for St. Stephen's Day." He glanced to his aunt. "Do you intend to go with the others?"

"I believe someone must go along to chaperone the ladies," she confided. "Moreover, I wish to observe Fitzwilliam with Miss Bennet in a situation beyond the sitting room."

Unfortunately, for both him and the countess, when they joined the ladies in the front parlor, a few minutes later, Miss Bennet informed them that she would not be a part of the outing.

Darcy was thankfully, however, to view Georgiana and Miss Davidson seated with Miss Bennet at a large table covered with a variety of greens: ivy, holly, pine, fir, sprigs of mistletoe, along with ribbons of every color.

"What have we here?" Darcy asked as he watched Miss Bennet guiding Georgiana's hands as his sister bent an evergreen limb to form a basket.

"Miss Bennet is showing us how to make a basket from the branches. I thought we might make one for each of the tenants—add a toy for the children and apples for the whole family. Miss Davidson is tying the joints together with string and finishing the basket off with a ribbon."

Miss Davidson added, "I cannot wait to share the idea with my mother. Mrs. Davidson will embrace the charitable elements of the presentation."

"The children could use the baskets to keep trinkets in or to nestle a pet," Georgiana said with enthusiasm.

Miss Bennet appeared pleased, but she cautioned, "Obviously, my father's estate was smaller than is Pemberley, and there were five of us to make the baskets."

"We could ask Mrs. Reynolds to assist," Georgiana suggested.

Darcy shot a glance to Miss Bennet, and the lady lifted an eyebrow in challenge. Surprisingly, instead of being irritated at her, he found himself smiling. "As Miss Bennet has indicated, mayhap there is not enough time to create baskets for each child upon the estate, even one per family would be more than one hundred and fifty."

His sister's smile dropped.

Yet, Darcy was quick to add, "Perhaps, this year, you can create the baskets for the different rooms at Pemberley."

When Georgiana's countenance still held disappointment, Miss Bennet suggested, "My sisters and I learned how to make the baskets from Mrs. Williamson, the local vicar's wife. Mrs. Williamson made the baskets, although larger, for the church during the Christmastide services. Her baskets held several candles, and, on Christmas's eve and Christmas day, she added flowers and occasionally large bows made of colorful ribbon." The lady looked to him for his approval of her words. "Do you think, sir, the church in Lambton would welcome the baskets if your sister and I made larger ones?"

"Making a half dozen for the church would be more practical than a hundred smaller ones," Darcy encouraged. "If you still wish to honor those at Pemberley, mayhap you could make smaller ones for the families of Pemberley's staff, many of whom have relations in the village and surrounding farms."

Georgiana said wistfully, "I like the idea of making the baskets for the church. Such sounds of something of which our father would have approved, do you not agree, William?"

Darcy looked lovingly on his sister, who was the image of their mother. "George Darcy would be bursting with pride at this moment, as am I."

Their cousin appeared at the drawing room door. "Bingley and Captain Stewart are having the sleighs brought around. If you ladies mean to go with us, you should gather your heavy cloaks, gloves, shawls, and muffs. We will leave in a quarter hour.

Georgiana turned to Miss Bennet. "Would you mind, ma'am, if we finished the baskets later?"

Miss Bennet smiled easily on his sister. "Naturally, our project can wait."

With a quick curtsey, Georgiana and Miss Davidson left the room, arm-in-arm.

Darcy turned to his cousin's betrothed. "You really should join them, Miss Bennet."

She did not look at him when she confessed, "My sharing a sleigh ride with my father was one of the last times we were together before he passed. Silly as it sounds, even after five years, the memory is too fresh."

"I am certain the colonel would have chosen a different activity if my cousin had knowledge of your sadness," Darcy assured. He wished desperately to reach out to her and pull the lady into his embrace to offer his comfort.

"There is no need for all to suffer because I am a sentimental daughter of an English gentleman," she said in tones that mocked her grief as insignificant.

"What will you do instead?" he asked. "Hopefully, you do not mean to spend your afternoon in the nursery. You have been invited to Pemberley for a holiday, ma'am. Such was Fitzwilliam's wish."

"Is this your way, sir, to remind me not to interfere in the affairs of your household?" she asked. An odd expression, one Darcy could not define, marked her features.

"Nonsense," Darcy argued. "Surely you must know, ma'am, I would do anything to view my cousin happy. The war has played heavy on him, and, if coming to Pemberley at Christmastide brings him solace, I welcome his presence here, and that includes those with whom he wishes to share his days."

"Share his days with Captain Stewart and me, you mean?" she asked softly. "I do not want to repeat myself, sir, but I cannot help but to feel uncomfortable to place you in a position of inconvenience, especially as you and the countess have shown me such remarkable kindness. Before the colonel's offer, my future appeared quite bleak, but I have discovered true humanity within the walls of Pemberley at a time of our God's greatest gift to the world. It is all quite unbelievable."

Darcy found himself moving closer to her, even considering taking her into his arms to provide comfort. Her eyes widened as if she knew what he was thinking, and he could view her recognition of his desires within hers before they clouded over, stopping his progress. Feeling awkward, he said, "You must learn to accept that you are safe at Pemberley. The colonel would not have brought you here if he thought otherwise."

Chapter Ten

Darcy had purposely seen the sleigh party off, stealing a private moment with Georgiana to tell her how much he appreciated her efforts with Miss Bennet. "Placing your desires aside proves you have grown into an exceptional woman."

"I simply took your advice," she whispered as a blush crept across her cheeks. "I decided it was not Miss Bennet's fault if she had engaged the colonel's heart and I had not."

Darcy thought his sister's reasoning would also serve him well, but he made no such comment aloud. Instead, he asked as he adjusted his sister's cloak about her shoulders. "And how did you find the lady?"

"My instincts, as did yours, tell me she is without guise, and, although I am sad at the loss of my cousin's attentions, the object of his affection is someone I might truly learn to admire."

After the party departed, with his sister choosing to ride with Captain Stewart, rather than with Edward and the countess, Darcy met briefly with Mrs. Reynolds regarding the St. Stephen's Day preparations, which, as he knew it would be, was a matter of futility, for he held no doubts regarding his housekeeper's efficiency. Rather, he had felt guilty for speaking a lie to his aunt about the need to oversee the event with his staff.

"Will there be anything else, sir?" his long-time servant asked.

"I assume you made arrangements for refreshments for the countess's party when they return."

"Yes, sir."

Darcy did not wish to ask, but he did so, nevertheless. "What of the Hursts and Miss Bennet?"

"To the best of my knowledge, Mr. and Mrs. Hurst remain in their quarters."

Darcy could hear the disapproval in his housekeeper's tone. He agreed: The Hursts were a useless plague on society—the very worst type, for the pair lived an indolent life and often sought other households upon which to impose in order to keep their own household expenses at a minimum. "And Miss Bennet? Please tell me the lady did not return to the nursery."

"Miss Bennet is in the portrait gallery. Earlier, when I discovered her there, I pointed out the images of your mother and father, as well as that of Miss Darcy."

"Did the lady approve of your providing her a 'tour' of this family's history?" he asked with a smile. He knew Mrs. Reynolds prided herself on sharing the splendor of Pemberley with others.

As expected, his housekeeper tilted her chin upward. "You know how loyal I am to this family."

Darcy's smile widened. "And I am blessed by the fact." He knew he should not ask—should not show so much attention to one of his guests, but he simply could not resist Miss Bennet's appeal. It was as if she were the candle's flame and he the moth. "Do you suppose the lady is still in the gallery?"

"I imagine so. Miss Bennet said something about fetching her sketchbook so she might practice drawing facial features. She said, often, she is expected to instruct her young charges regarding such matters."

* * *

In the gallery there were many family portraits, but she admitted, if only to herself, they had little to fix the attention of a stranger. She had enjoyed those moments spent earlier with Mrs. Reynolds, and Elizabeth had respectfully listened to the woman's tales of the current family, but, in truth, she wished only to look upon one particular portrait.

Returning to the gallery with her sketchbook and pencils, Elizabeth walked in quest of the only face whose features she wished to look upon. At last, she came to stand before a striking resemblance to Mr. Darcy, although it was a much younger version of the man she had come to know and admire. In the portrait, Mr. Darcy sported the same smile she had occasionally observed upon his lips when he looked upon her. She wondered if he looked at others in the same manner and exactly what he thought of her when he watched her so closely.

"Let us see if I can capture the essence of the man. I would like to carry the image with me when I must depart Pemberley."

Therefore, she had been at the task some twenty minutes when the subject of her unaccounted-for interest appeared at the other end of the gallery.

They were within twenty yards of each other, and so abrupt was his appearance that it was impossible to avoid his finding her before his portrait. Their eyes met briefly, and the cheeks of both were overspread with the deepest blush. He started, and, for a moment, seemed immovable, but the gentleman quickly recovered himself and advanced toward her.

Elizabeth had briefly turned away, quickly closing her sketchbook. Embarrassed to have been caught attempting to capture his likeness. She thought quickly to make her excuses; yet, as he drew nearer, she dared lift her eyes to meet his steady gaze. "Mr. Darcy, this is a surprise," she managed to say.

"A surprise that I might choose to visit my own gallery or to cross it to reach a different part of the house?" he asked, as he slowed his approach.

Elizabeth had instinctively dropped her eyes. "I meant no offense, sir."

Mr. Darcy stopped short of where she stood. "No reprimand was intended, Miss Bennet. I sometimes forget the tone of my voice, especially when speaking to those who do not know me well, can sometimes be construed as off-putting, when, in reality, I meant my words to be an easy taunt."

She glanced up at him shyly. "Perhaps you might add a smile when you are simply stating the facts as you know them or are speaking in an intended jest. In that manner, people would know your intentions."

The gentleman said softly, "It has been some time since I have had reason to smile in a genuine manner."

Elizabeth quickly regretted her gentle tease. "Naturally, my foolishly-worded reprimand was untimely. You have been in mourning since your wife's passing. It was ill-considerate of me to offer a reproof where none was required. My mother always told me to hold my tongue, but I often forget those lessons. I sincerely apologize, sir."

"My greatest regret with Anne's passing is I am deeply sorry that Cassandra will grow into adulthood without her mother. My daughter will be just like my sweet Georgiana, who suffered greatly with the loss of our mother," he admitted.

"I did not realize Miss Darcy lost her mother so early," Elizabeth said as she innately reached out a hand to squeeze his forearm in comfort. "How old were you when the previous Mrs. Darcy passed? It must have been equally as hard upon you, as it was for your sister."

"I am twelve years Miss Darcy's senior," he said in melancholy, a feeling, which, obviously, embarrassed him.

"I have upset you again," Elizabeth said with self-reproach. "You should tell me your family is none of my concern. I truly shan't be offended if you do."

Mr. Darcy looked upon her with softness; it was the same look as she had noted previously in his portrait. "You are the first person in many years who has asked of my feelings," he admitted.

"Surely your father permitted you time to grieve your mother," she demanded.

"I loved my father with a fierceness I have never been able to explain to another. However, after my mother's death, it was as if he heard death's knell ringing above his head, and all he planned for me had taken on an unexplained urgency. He became not only my father but also my mentor. He began to instruct me on the running of Pemberley with an intensity that many, including me, have questioned over the years. He taught me the nuances of business negotiations and tenant contracts. Of my obligations to Miss Darcy. Of every aspect of my life, except, perhaps, how to choose a proper bride." He sighed heavily. "Everything except—" He paused suddenly.

Elizabeth added, "Except how to love another."

Mr. Darcy did not respond for several elongated moments. "I was eighteen before I realized my father's 'sharpness' came from the fact he never forgave himself for my mother's death. Lady Anne Darcy died from childbed fever, as did my wife." He paused to shake his head in irony. "Both Mrs. Darcys were named Anne."

"I understand," she said in sympathy. "My mother, Mrs. Bennet, blamed herself for not delivering a son to set aside the entailment on the family estate. For as long as I can recall, she promoted one or another of my sisters to every eligible gentleman within a twenty miles' radius of my father's estate, for fear of what could happen if my father died early on. Then Mr. Bennet had a spell with his heart and was gone before any of us could claim a second thought on what to do. My mother's worst nightmare arrived with a vengeance. We were all turned out by my father's cousin. Making matters worse, one of my dearest friends replaced my mother as the estate's mistress. Mrs. Bennet's ire doubled against me, for it was my fault all of my dear family lost their home and place in society."

"How could what happened after your father's untimely death be your fault?" he demanded.

"My father's death was the fault of no one, except the call of God's angel for Mr. Bennet's early departure from this earth," she explained, "but the displacement of my family, most assuredly, falls upon my shoulders. You see, before proposing to my friend, Miss Lucas, my father's cousin proposed to me." Like Mr. Darcy, she shook her head in irony. "On the exact same day as he proposed to Charlotte—in fact, only hours apart."

"Then the man did not hold you in affection?" Mr. Darcy asked in apparent concern.

"I do not believe my cousin felt anything for Miss Lucas either, although when I spent time with them the spring before Mr. Bennet's passing, they had carved out a suitable arrangement in their marriage. Miss Lucas is older than I and did not wish to be a burden to her family, and so, she accepted her one and only proposal in order to claim a house of her own. At the time, my cousin held a respectable living as a clergyman."

"Do you truly regret refusing your cousin's proposal?" he asked in sincere tones.

"Not for myself," she admitted, "but, most assuredly, for my mother and sisters. I have placed them in a life of servitude and of living off the graciousness of my mother's relations. Such is the reason I quickly took a position as a governess. I wished to relieve the burden placed upon my Uncle Gardiner, who took in my two eldest sisters and me. It was the best I could do after ruining Jane's and Mary's future."

* * *

With a nod of acceptance of what she said of her family and the reason for her reduced circumstances, Darcy had offered her his arm. "Permit me to introduce you to my relations."

She smiled up at him with that mischievous smile he had observed often on her lips the last few days. "Am I to be the recipient of a tour of Pemberley's gallery by the master himself?"

"Do you object, Miss Bennet?" he said with a lightheartedness he had not felt in more than a dozen years.

"I am honored, sir."

Therefore, for the next hour, Darcy had led her about the gallery, relating stories his father had repeated to him on multiple occasions, assuring that Darcy could speak the storied history of the Darcy family to his own children.

Without prompting, Miss Bennet had recognized how he favored his father's cousin Samuel. Even more remarkable, but something that greatly pleased him, the lady knew something of Samuel Darcy's life's work, having read two different papers, which had once been a part of her father's library, on his Cousin Samuel's discovery of an ancient Egyptian civilization. Darcy knew few men who could converse intelligently on Cousin Samuel's work. To do so with a woman had nearly had him acting against the warning constantly reminding him the lady was not designed for him.

They had parted when her abigail, Hannah, had come to fetch her. Miss Bennet had promised Hurst's sons another story of Wellington's victories, and so, she had gathered her pencils and sketchbook, made her apologies, and left him alone with his memories of his parents, his ancestors, and the most fetching woman Darcy had ever encountered.

* * *

"To whom are you writing?" Lady Matlock asked.

The sleigh riders had returned, changed out of their damp clothing, and reconvened in his aunt's favorite drawing room for tea and biscuits. Still a bit consumed by his thoughts upon the time he had spent with Miss Bennet, Darcy had found a place at the small desk in the corner of the room to write to Anne's mother. Lady Catherine enjoyed the tales he shared of Cassandra's "achievements." Therefore, he dutifully wrote to his aunt every few weeks.

"To Aunt Catherine," he stated flatly. However, he noted how Miss Bennet smiled as she tended her needlework. When she had asked about a portrait of Anne, he had explained how Anne wanted to wait until after her lying in, how Anne favored her father more than her mother, and how he regularly kept her ladyship informed of how her granddaughter fared.

Miss Bingley observed, "Mr. Darcy's handwriting is always so exact, nothing like Charles's. It is a pleasure to read one of your letters, sir."

"One of Darcy's letters to Bingley, you mean," the countess was quick to correct the impression that he and Miss Bingley were intimates, while attempting to keep her apparent dislike for Miss Bingley absent from her tone. "It would not be proper for my nephew to write to a woman not his betrothed or a relative."

"Naturally, I meant one of my brother's letters," Miss Bingley said in what sounded of petulance. The woman turned to him, purposely ignoring the unspoken reprimand the countess had delivered. In truth, Darcy was surprised she would dare to address him again after their last exchange of bitter words; however, her doing so spoke to her desperation. As far as he knew, Miss Bingley had had only the one proposal, which she had refused, thinking Darcy might make an offer to her after Anne's passing. She would be, most assuredly, waiting for an eternity, if she expected him to extend his hand to her. He could no longer put off the talk with Bingley: He would call his friend into his study and inform Bingley that he would no longer receive the man's sisters. Any invitations Bingley received from Darcy were for him alone. Miss Bingley cleared her throat before speaking to him in a coquettish tone, which did not suit her, "You write uncommonly fast, Mr. Darcy."

Without looking up, Darcy said in a deadpan manner. "You are mistaken; I write rather slowly."

Again, Miss Bingley ignored his lack of enthusiasm for the conversation. "How many letters you must have occasion to write in the course of a year! Letters of business, too! How odious I should think them!"

He refused to look at her when he responded. "It is fortunate, then, that they fall to my lot instead of yours."

His aunt said, "Tell Catherine that Matlock and I plan to visit with her at the end of March for several days. We will bring Miss Ashley to take her ladyship's acquaintance."

"I have already told her so once, as you mentioned your plans the evening I took Miss Ashley's acquaintance, as I assumed it would be your desire," he said with a smile for Lady Matlock. "Such was your order to your eldest son and me at the ball last week."

"You are more attentive to all I say than are either of my sons," Lady Matlock said with a challenging lift of an eyebrow in the colonel's direction.

Edward chuckled good-naturedly. "Selective hearing has always served me well in both my personal life and my military career," he declared. "As for my visiting Aunt Catherine, you know I only call in at Kent when Darcy is there to serve as a shield, deflecting Aunt Catherine's chastisements to me. Moreover, it is Roland's turn to visit with her ladyship. I traveled with Darcy to escort Anne's body to her childhood home. A grieving Aunt Catherine is worse than her ladyship's customary complaints."

Lady Matlock presented her son a warning. "When your father and I travel to Kent, I shall expect your company." The countess looked pointedly to Miss Bennet before returning her gaze to her son. The colonel appeared oblivious to the meaning and simply returned to his conversation with Georgiana, but Darcy had noticed and understood: Fitzwilliam would be escorting his new bride to meet Lady Catherine.

Miss Bingley grabbed the opportunity of the reprimand to reestablish herself as the center of attention. "Do you always write such charming long letters to your aunt, Mr. Darcy?"

He again glanced down at the letter before him, refusing to look at the woman. "They are generally long, but whether always charming, it is not for me to determine."

Miss Bingley declared, "It is a rule with me, that a person who can write a long letter with ease cannot write ill."

Bingley must have finally understood Darcy's displeasure, for his friend jokingly said, "That will not do for a compliment to Darcy, Caroline, because he does not write with ease. He studies too much for words of four syllables. Do you not, Darcy?"

Darcy found himself frowning at what had begun as a reprimand for Miss Bingley, but had ended with a taunt directed at him. "My style of writing is very different from yours," he managed to say without emotion marking his tone.

"Oh," cried Miss Bingley, "Charles writes in the most careless way imaginable. He leaves out half of his words and blots the rest." As usual, the lady defended Darcy in hopes of earning his loyalty. Such would not happen in Darcy's lifetime.

Bingley, customarily easy of temperament, simply grinned widely. "My ideas flow so rapidly that I have not time to express them, which means my letters sometimes convey no ideas at all to my correspondents."

Miss Bennet joined the conversation, and Darcy's full attention was finally captured. "Your humility, Mr. Bingley, must disarm proof."

Darcy smiled kindly on the lady, and he spoke as if sharing an idea with her alone. "Nothing is more deceitful than the appearance of humility. It is often only carelessness of opinion and sometimes an indirect boast."

"And which of the two do you call my little recent piece of modesty?" Bingley demanded.

Darcy set his pen in its holder. "The indirect boast, for you are really proud of your defects in writing, because you consider them as proceeding from a rapidity of thought and careless execution, which, if not estimable, you think, at least, interesting. The power of doing anything with quickness is always much prized by the possessor and often without any attention to the imperfection of the performance. When you told Miss Whalen earlier that if you ever resolved on quitting a place, you should be gone in five minutes, you meant your remark to be a sort of panegyric, a compliment to yourself; and, yet, what is there so laudable in a precipitance which must leave necessary business undone and be no real advantage to yourself or anyone else?"

"Nay," cried Bingley, "this is too much to remember in the late afternoon all that I said in the morning. And, yet, upon my honor, I believe what I said of myself to be true, and I believe it at this moment. At least, therefore, I did not assume the character of needless precipitance merely to exhibit before the ladies."

Darcy nodded his head in acceptance before saying, "I dare say you believed it, but I am by no means convinced that you would be gone with such celerity. Your conduct would be quite dependent on chance as that of any man I know; and, if, as you were mounting your horse, a friend were to say, 'Bingley, you had better stay till next week,' you would probably do it—you would probably not go—and, at another word, might stay a month."

Several in the room nodded their agreement, and Captain Stewart jovially slapped Bingley on the back. However, it was Miss Bennet who protested, but with that grin on her lips that Darcy was coming to adore.

"You have only proved by this that Mr. Bingley did not do justice to his own disposition," the lady asserted. "You have shown him off now much more than he did himself."

"Miss Bennet is correct, Darcy," the colonel said from where he sat with Georgiana, who watched the conversation with an interest Darcy could not identify.

Bingley rushed to claim the glory presented him by the lady. "I am exceedingly gratified, Miss Bennet, by your converting what my friend says into a compliment on the sweetness of my temper. But I am afraid you are giving it a turn which that gentleman did by no means intend; for he certainly would think better of me if, under such a circumstance, I were to give a flat denial and ride off as fast as I could."

Miss Bennet asked, "Would Mr. Darcy then consider the rashness of your original intentions as atoned for by your obstinacy in adhering to it?"

"Upon my word I cannot exactly explain the matter. Darcy must explain for himself," Bingley insisted.

Darcy frowned. He did not approve of Bingley's response. He knew his friend avoided confrontation of any kind, but he had simply been speaking the truth, as he saw it. "You expect me to account for opinions which you choose to call mine, but I have not acknowledged. Allowing the case, however, to stand according to your representation, you must understand, Miss Bennet, that the friend who is supposed to desire his return to the house, and the delay of his plan, has merely desired it, asked it without offering one argument in favor of its propriety."

The conversation started by the countess regarding his letter had transformed into a "private" one between him and Miss Bennet.

She cleared her throat, as if considering her words, before asking, "To yield readily—easily—to the persuasion of a 'friend' has no merit with you?"

Darcy felt as if they no longer spoke of Bingley's lack of resolve, but rather her agreement with his cousin. Weighing what she had disclosed earlier about how her decision to refuse her father's cousin's offer of his hand had changed the trajectory of each of her sisters' lives, as well as that of her mother, had Darcy thinking perhaps she meant to rectify her 'wrongs' by securing a connection to the earldom with her agreement to Edward's proposal. Mayhap, the colonel and the lady were not simply keeping their arrangement secret, as Darcy and the countess had suspected. Perhaps they were keeping secrets for other reasons. It was time for Darcy to have another talk with his cousin.

Darcy took time to consider his response before speaking. It would fit either situation. "To yield without conviction is no compliment to the understanding of either involved."

Chapter eleven

Ironically, Darcy had no need to seek out his cousin, for Fitzwilliam cornered him after supper while the other men enjoyed their cheroots and brandy. They stood together near the bank of windows at the back of the room and looked out on the snow-encrusted lawn.

The colonel asked softly, "What was all that give-and-take with Miss Bennet this evening, Darcy? If I did not know better, I would think you were flirting with the lady."

Darcy knew he frowned, but he could not quite keep the expression from his features. "Most assuredly, I would never openly woo a woman across a drawing room with an audience in attendance."

"Have you ever 'wooed' a woman in private, Cousin?" Fitzwilliam asked with a grin.

"Do not forget I have been married," Darcy countered.

The colonel ignored Darcy's example. "You never wooed your wife. Lady Catherine badgered both you and Anne until you two conceded defeat. Neither of you knew the first blush of romance or even the last blush, for that matter."

"My marriage to Anne is a closed subject," Darcy warned.

"I never understood why you gave sway to our aunt," Fitzwilliam admitted.

They stood in companionable silence for several minutes before Darcy ventured, "Setting your observations on my life aside, tell me what happens to Miss Bennet after Christmastide."

The colonel continued to look out upon the night, but he answered, nevertheless. "I suppose the lady's future depends on us. Upon my family."

"You mean your promise to the lady?"

His cousin shrugged in feigned nonchalance, but Darcy knew Fitzwilliam would be greatly moved by any act of honor on his part. The colonel considered his word as a bond. "I had hoped Miss Bennet could prove herself to all of my family. From what I observed earlier, I thought you had taken a liking to the lady."

Darcy readily admitted, "I have. I find Miss Bennet very amiable and exceptionally intelligent." He did not say more, for fear of exposing his true thoughts.

"Then you and the countess will do as I ask and assist her?"

Darcy glanced to the others, who were preparing to join the ladies. "Naturally, if such is your genuine wish, you have my full support."

* * *

Thursday, 24 December 1818

As Elizabeth pinned the small piece of lace to her most serviceable day dress, using her grandmother's brooch to anchor it in place, she made her decision to speak to the colonel about an idea that had been brewing in her mind since her last encounter with Mrs. Henry. Wishing to hear the gentleman's opinion, she rushed below, hoping to find Colonel Fitzwilliam in the morning room.

"Good morning, Miss Bennet," the countess said as Elizabeth entered.

Elizabeth paused to curtsey. "Good morning, my lady." She glanced about the room and knew instant disappointment not to find the colonel within.

Lady Matlock said, "You appear to be searching for someone, my dear."

"I had hoped to speak to your son, my lady," Elizabeth admitted.

The countess smiled easily. "Fitzwilliam is generally very prompt. I expect him any moment. Come join me until he arrives."

Elizabeth would have preferred to be alone so she could review her idea once more, but she thanked Lady Matlock and moved to the sidebar to claim toast and a coddled egg.

"What may I bring you to drink, miss?" Mr. Nathan asked as he seated her.

"Tea, please."

Within seconds, her teacup was full, and she was presented her privacy with the countess. "Are you enjoying your stay at Pemberley, Miss Bennet?"

"Who could not, my lady?" Elizabeth spoke in appreciative tones. "It is all quite grand. I must admit being here, even for this brief interlude, has greatly boosted my spirits. Your kindness, as well as that of Mr. Darcy, is beyond compare."

"There is no need for praise, my dear. We are happy to assist in any means possible," her ladyship declared. "It is quite unusual for Fitzwilliam to bring someone to Derbyshire to take our acquaintance, especially someone of whom we held no prior knowledge. We do not object to your presence here; therefore, do not think my remark is meant as criticism, rather, it is an observation. Generally, when Fitzwilliam visits, he comes alone or with one of his fellow officers. I can honestly say, my youngest son has never presented me the acquaintance of a young lady."

Elizabeth said honestly, "I, too, was surprised by the colonel's offer, especially as our acquaintance was of a short duration."

Before more could be said, the subject of their conversation strolled into the room, pausing briefly to bow to them. "Two of my favorite ladies," the colonel said with his customary smile. He crossed quickly to buss his mother's upturned cheek with a kiss. "You are both up exceptionally early."

"I promised Darcy I would finalize the seating for the supper preceding the New Year's ball. The addition of Mr. and Mrs. Hurst and Miss Bingley creates a problem. The numbers will be uneven and another leaf will be required in the table. Moreover, I must determine who to ask to join us for the meal. It must be someone local, for many rooms at Pemberley are not available unless Darcy wishes to hire additional staff for the event."

"There are too few days before the ball," the colonel observed. "If I were Darcy, I would refuse the attendance of Bingley's family. It is definitely bad *ton* to invite oneself to an event." The colonel sat beside Elizabeth.

111

"If a room is required for another, I could remove to the room set aside for the governess," Elizabeth offered. "It would be no great bother for me to do so. Moreover, do not count me for the supper or the ball. I would never impose on a family tradition in such a manner."

The countess tutted her displeasure. "You shall do no such thing. Darcy and I will not tolerate your withdrawal, nor will my son. The colonel invited you to Pemberley in order that his family might learn more of your character. I think I can speak for Darcy when I say you have been a rare gem worth discovering. We are pleased to have you among us."

Elizabeth's heart swelled with gratefulness when she looked upon Lady Matlock. She had arrived at Pemberley not knowing what to expect and had found acceptance at every turn.

Her ladyship patted the back of Elizabeth's hand. "Now, I shall leave you two to your conversation before you are interrupted by the others. Inform me of your plans, Fitzwilliam, once you and the other gentlemen decide what your day holds."

"Yes, Mother," he repeated dutifully, as both he and Elizabeth stood to recognize the countess's withdrawal. Once they were seated again, the colonel remarked, "I am pleased to see how well you and my mother get along together."

"Her ladyship is truly a remarkable woman," Elizabeth said in honest tones. "Even if nothing comes from my time at Pemberley, as to another post, I cannot regret my decision to take advantage of your invitation, sir. Being here has bolstered my spirits for the future."

The colonel nodded his understanding. "I cannot tell you how often I have experienced a similar emotion. My years on the front with Wellington have, upon occasion, left me feeling devoid of hope for mankind. Then, I would return to England and to the bosom of my family long enough to heal, at least partially. Such was the reason I insisted you join us at Pemberley." He motioned Mr. Nathan to refill her tea. "I would be happy to continue this easy conversation, but was there something specific you wished to discuss?"

Elizabeth waited until Mr. Nathan stepped away from the table before she spoke. She said softly, "Do you recall when Mrs. Henry brought me this circle of lace?"

The colonel eyed the cloth. "I do."

Elizabeth again looked to Mr. Nathan to assure some degree of privacy before continuing. "I was wondering how your cousin, Mr. Darcy, would act if I approached him with an idea on how to assist Mrs. Henry and others among his tenants."

"I thought you already assisted Darcy with Mrs. Henry's farm. Something about a young man and his wife taking over the running of the farm by residing with Mrs. Henry."

"I did, but Mr. Darcy, obviously, considered the situation only a temporary solution to the issues for both Mrs. Henry and Mr. Braun."

"And you possess a more permanent solution?" the colonel inquired.

"Perhaps," Elizabeth said, still not certain she should interfere. "Mrs. Henry said she and others on the estate could make lace of good quality."

The colonel frowned. "I know I said the swatch of lace presented to you was what I would consider to be of good quality, but a group of women in Derbyshire will not be able to compete with the factories in Manchester and Liverpool."

"It is not necessary for them to *compete*," Elizabeth argued. "Despite the efficiency of the mills, there will always be a market for handmade, one-of-a-kind products. What I am suggesting is for your cousin to develop a market for his cottagers' product or products."

"Not the reverse—the product for the market?" The colonel smiled widely. "You must permit me to be in the room when you approach my cousin."

Elizabeth worried her bottom lip with her teeth. "I do not wish to offend Mr. Darcy."

The colonel declared, "I assure you Darcy will claim no offense, while he will likely be quite prudish in his initial response. The late George Darcy taught my cousin that his opinions are absolutes, but Darcy is not without the ability to reason. You must not be afraid of his tone or what I always call his 'eagle-eye' stare."

Elizabeth chuckled nervously. "Mayhap, I should simply keep my opinions to myself."

"Oh, no," the colonel protested. "I believe this discussion would be an excellent lesson for all involved."

Before Elizabeth could lodge a protest of her own, Mr. Darcy entered the morning room. When he spotted her and the colonel together, the gentleman frowned, causing Elizabeth to sink deeper into her chair.

"Morning, Cousin, please join us," the colonel called.

Mr. Darcy said stiffly, "I would not wish to interrupt your conversation with Miss Bennet. I simply came to ask Mr. Nathan to prepare me a plate and bring it to my study."

The colonel appeared to study his cousin carefully before saying, "Then, I am assuming you are too busy to have a private meeting with Miss Bennet and me."

* * *

Darcy's stomach turned upside down, his hunger driven away by the vision of Miss Bennet sitting beside his cousin, their heads together in private conversation. "I have a busy schedule," he said. "After all, it is Christmas Eve."

"I had forgotten the day," Miss Bennet admitted. "Certainly, you hold responsibilities to the estate. Our conversation can wait."

Darcy thought he had avoided watching the colonel and Miss Bennet together until his cousin said, "The days after Christmas will become more hectic with the arrival of the other guests. If you could provide us a quarter hour, we promise we will be concise."

Darcy sighed internally. "As you wish, Fitzwilliam." Without providing Mr. Nathan his instructions, he turned on his heels and left the room.

* * *

"That was odd," Elizabeth remarked, her eyes still on the open door.

"If I did not know better—" the colonel began, but did not finish his thought.

"Mr. Darcy appeared from sort," Elizabeth observed. "Is that what you meant by the late Mr. Darcy's lessons on negotiations?"

"I suppose we should discover that fact for ourselves. If you are finished with your meal, we should speak to Darcy before my cousin changes his mind and puts us off."

He rose then and offered her his hand to assist her to her feet. Before she accepted, Elizabeth shot another wary glance to the door through which Mr. Darcy had made his exit. "As you say, sir."

* * *

Darcy knew he was being foolish. His response was simply his heart revolting at the scene he had encountered in his morning room: Miss Bennet and Fitzwilliam alone and talking privately. "Dear God," he said as another thought froze him in place, "do not permit Edward to ask me to stand up with him or to ask permission to announce his engagement at the New Year's ball." He squeezed his eyes shut to drive away the image of the pair in a locked embrace, when he quickly became aware of their approach in the hall. Darcy managed to sit behind his desk and to take up his pen before Fitzwilliam led Miss Bennet into the room.

He motioned them forward and returned the pen to its holder. Once they were seated, he said with as much calm as he could muster, "How might I assist you, Fitzwilliam?" Darcy kept his gaze on his cousin, rather than on the woman who had beguiled him with her charm.

His cousin said, "Actually, the need to speak to you was Miss Bennet's idea, and, as the lady is more than capable of speaking for herself, I will claim a supporting role in this gathering."

Whether he wished it or not, Darcy turned his attention to the woman whose presence had haunted his dreams since the day she walked through Pemberley's door. After his talk with Fitzwilliam last evening, Darcy had fallen asleep, conjuring up his favorite dream of kissing the lady, which customarily led to him taking her to his bed. However, in last night's dream, they had been interrupted by his cousin—the result being a physical fight between him and Fitzwilliam, one so real that it had jolted Darcy from his sleep. The echo of Fitzwilliam calling him a "traitor" still rang in his ears.

Miss Bennet cleared her throat. "I fear, Mr. Darcy, I am assuming too much latitude in approaching you on this subject, but I cannot seem to forget Mrs. Henry's situation."

Dumbfounded by not hearing the dreaded words that would steal her away from him forever, Darcy found himself staring at her in disbelief. At length, blinking away his confusion, he asked, "Mrs.

Henry? I thought we had settled that lady's place at Pemberley to your satisfaction. I assure you, Miss Bennet, I cannot favor Mrs. Henry further. If so, all my tenants would expect the same."

"Most assuredly, sir, I am not advocating for you to discover other means to aid Mrs. Henry's continued presence at her family farm. I am not so foolish as to think such would not eventually ruin your estate."

"Then for what have you become the champion, Miss Bennet?" Darcy was so glad not to be discussing his cousin's marriage to the lady, he leaned forward to listen more carefully.

"If you please, sir, permit me to preface my suggestion with an explanation of how I came by the knowledge that I wish to share with you."

Darcy nodded his permission and simply claimed the pleasure of looking upon the woman he had come to adore. Ironically, he no longer saw his cousin at the lady's side: In his mind, Darcy conversed with Miss Bennet. The subject matter held no importance—just the two of them enjoying an exchange of ideas.

She continued, "Some six months before his passing, Mr. Bennet began to explore additional means to increase the profit of our home estate. At the time, the war still reigned, and England was stepping away from its agricultural roots."

Darcy remarked, "The draw of the industrial towns is a constant botheration for the aristocracy."

Miss Bennet nodded her agreement. "The problem has become more complicated with the end of the war." She glanced to Fitzwilliam and smiled. "The colonel can tell you better than I of the problems many soldiers are having locating steady employment. One of the men the Sample family hired when I was employed by them had spent six years in the army and service to his country. Before that, he had worked in the fabric industry. I am not certain what he had done before the army, but his weaving skills were no longer viable after the war. In the years of his absence, everything he knew of the fabric industry had changed."

"What has this to do with Mrs. Henry?" Darcy asked, still confused as to the point Miss Bennet wished to make.

The lady blushed easily. "I do apologize. I digressed." She reached for the pin on her dress and released the latch. Palming the pin, she handed him the circle of lace. "Mrs. Henry presented me this lace in gratitude for my efforts to calm her before she spoke to you. The colonel was with me when the woman called on me."

Darcy now realized what his cousin had meant when the colonel told the countess he had been speaking of lace, but Darcy wished it had been him available to greet Mrs. Henry, along with Miss Bennet.

The lady continued, "My uncle, sir, owns an import and export business. I know a good deal more about lace than do many. Even without much prompting, as a businessman, you must realize there is a market for both handmade lace and machine-made lace."

"And what do you propose?" Darcy demanded. "That I set Mrs. Henry to making lace to pay her rents? I doubt if the lady could produce enough to make such a suggestion profitable."

"Most assuredly, she could not do so on her own. Not alone," she challenged. "But Mrs. Henry says there are many more on Pemberley estate who are experts with a needle." She sighed heavily. "What I did not explain earlier is my father invested in a breed of sheep whose wool was in great demand, along with encouraging several artisans who were handy with cabinet-making to expand their craft. Mr. Bennet did not live long enough to know whether his scheme increased profits for the estate and the workers, but I cannot see how it could hurt to explore all possibilities. My uncle was to assist in placing the cabinets and desks in prominent shops and London homes. My father hoped doing so would keep the estate solvent."

Darcy weighed what she said. "Develop products in demand by finer households. Interesting idea."

"Not necessarily an original one," Miss Bennet said simply. "Men such as Josiah Wedgewood realized the middle class had money to spend, and they wanted to emulate their betters. He made cheaper versions of pottery styles imported from China. Even so, Wedgewood also has his exclusive line in his showroom in London."

Darcy said with enthusiasm, "Instead of fretting over the demise of the landed gentry, we develop other means to combat the loss. I am grieved your father did not live to view whether his plans knew success or not. I would have enjoyed taking the acquaintance of such a man, Miss Bennet."

"I am certain, even with Papa's sometimes quirky outlook, he would have been impressed by all you and your family have achieved, Mr. Darcy. If nothing else, you could have placed him in your library and forgot about him, for he would never have chosen to leave."

Darcy chuckled, "He sounds like a man I would have respected." He noted how Miss Bennet's bottom lip began to tremble, but before he could offer his comfort, his cousin joined the conversation.

Fitzwilliam appeared as surprised as had been Darcy as to what Miss Bennet had proposed. "The lady is much more than a governess. Do you not think so, Darcy?"

"She is indeed," Darcy said in admiration. "Would you mind waiting a few minutes, Miss Bennet, while I send for my land steward?"

His cousin noted, "It is the day before Christmas, Darcy."

"I know," Darcy announced, "but I want Mr. Stanley to speak to Mrs. Henry and gather the names of others who we might employ. We will also require a place for the work to take place." He stood to look down on Miss Bennet. "You say your uncle might assist us?"

The lady blushed again. "I cannot speak a guarantee, but I will gladly write to him on your behalf."

Chapter twelve

Darcy had been so relieved not to be called upon to congratulate his cousin, he had rushed from the room to send a message to his steward. Miss Bennet's idea had been a rudimentary one, but it had demonstrated how absolutely perfect she was for him, and, although a part of his being rejected the idea of the lady being married to Fitzwilliam, at a minimum, Darcy could recognize her generous nature by assuring her of her true worth. Moreover, if Fitzwilliam meant to leave his military duties behind and settle in Oxfordshire with the lady, his cousin would require a woman willing to assist in the colonel's transition to the land. The only problem Darcy foresaw with this idea was the likelihood of his never finding another to equal her.

After sending a footman to Mr. Stanley's cottage to ask the steward to call upon him, Darcy paused to answer several questions from Mrs. Reynolds and to send Mr. Nathan for that breakfast tray after all, and an order of tea for both Miss Bennet and the colonel.

Finished with his task, he rushed back to his study, only to be brought up short by the image of Miss Bennet studying a miniature on a side table in the area of the study that his father had, generally, used to meet with business associates and her words, "Oh, my, you are 'the' Mr. Darcy."

* * *

When Mr. Darcy departed the room, Elizabeth desperately wanted to present herself a congratulatory squeeze. Knowing she could not sit perfectly still, she asked the colonel, "Do you think your cousin would mind if I had a look about his study. I have been making sketches of figures in the portraits about the house, as well as designs on urns so I will have them for my next posting with a family."

"I cannot imagine Darcy would object," the colonel said in disinterest. "If you do not mind, I want to ask Mr. Nathan to send in a pot of tea and some biscuits. If I know my cousin, we will be here for more than a few minutes."

Elizabeth stood to make her way toward a portrait of a man she now recognized as George Darcy; this image was a much older version of the man she had viewed previously in the gallery. "Fresh tea would be welcomed," she murmured as she studied the likeness of the man looking down upon her. Foolish as it was to think it, she wondered what the elder Mr. Darcy would think of her blossoming feelings for his son. Would she be found wanting or would the "great man" approve of her? She supposed it would be the first, for she had no standing in society.

"My Uncle Darcy," the colonel explained.

"I recognize him," she admitted. "I have viewed the younger version of the gentleman, along with the other portraits in the gallery. When I saw the portrait of Mr. Samuel Darcy, I thought your cousin favored him, but now that I have seen this one of George Darcy, I realize your cousin's resemblance to his father is quite striking."

"Quite perceptive," the colonel admitted. "I had never noticed Darcy's resemblance to his Cousin Samuel, but I would agree." With a bow, he said, "Pardon me." And then he was gone.

Elizabeth studied the portrait for several minutes, imagining how handsome the current Mr. Darcy would be with a touch of grey at his temples. "Some woman will know the pleasure of the gentleman's company for the remainder of her days." She sighed in regret. "But not you, Elizabeth Bennet."

She forced herself to walk away from the portrait toward a display of miniatures, the first of which was of Miss Darcy as a young girl of perhaps ten. The girl's countenance displayed the potential of her beauty, which was now fully apparent for all the world to view. Elizabeth bent over for a closer look: It was at that moment, that she saw the image of a man she recognized. Despite knowing she should not touch it, she picked up the miniature for a closer look.

"Mr. Wickham," she whispered. "A most gentleman-like appearance. I remember the first time I laid eyes on the lieutenant on the streets of Meryton. I was with my sisters and Mr. Wickham accompanied his friend, Captain Denny. At the time, I thought the gentleman wanted only regimentals to make him completely charming." She mindlessly stroked the image with her fingertip as a myriad of memories flashed behind her eyes. Mr. Wickham was a part of the world she had left behind in Hertfordshire. "An appearance greatly in your favor, as you were well aware—all the best part of beauty—a fine countenance, a good figure, and a very pleasing address."

She heard what could only be the hurried steps of Mr. Darcy, and Elizabeth thought to return the miniature to its proper place; however, a connection to her host clicked in her brain and the subject of many of Mr. Wickham's complaints materialized before she could do more than say, "Oh, my, you are 'the' Mr. Darcy."

The gentleman in question frowned. "Pardon?"

Elizabeth blushed thoroughly, but she turned the miniature to where Mr. Darcy could view what she held. "I once held an acquaintance with Mr. Wickham, and I heard much of your and the gentleman's relationship from the lieutenant."

"I can easily imagine such was so," Mr. Darcy said in obvious irritation.

"I apologize, sir. I did not mean to intrude," she rushed to say. "While I waited for your and the colonel's return, I thought to look upon for your father's portrait, and then I noticed the image of Miss Darcy on this table." He had not yet stepped further into the room, and Elizabeth wondered if she had offended him greatly by snooping about the room.

"You said Mr. Wickham was a lieutenant?" he asked in that quiet form of control that she was beginning to realize was a part of his nature.

"Yes, in the local militia in Meryton in Hertfordshire. Near where my father's estate was located," she supplied.

"And that was?" he asked. Elizabeth noted how still he held himself, as if he expected someone to strike him, and she briefly wondered how he came to be so cautious of his feelings.

"More than five years past," she explained. "Obviously, before the war ended. The militia moved to Brighton about the same time as Mr. Bennet passed. I do not know what became of Lieutenant Wickham. None of my sisters have mentioned any of the local men involved in the militia at that time. I suppose the death of our father drove such frivolous thoughts from their heads. Mr. Bennet's passing required us all to consider more pressing matters."

"Mr. Wickham died in a duel. Another man shot him in the heart when he caught Wickham with his daughter."

Elizabeth glanced again to the image in her hand. "I am grieved to hear of his passing. He was too young to die, but, I can say honestly, I am not surprised by the incident. Mr. Wickham's attentions quickly turned to Miss King after the lady inherited a small fortune."

Mr. Darcy took several steps into the room, but he still appeared quite agitated. In fact, his demeanor spoke heavily of his unrest. "Mr. Wickham's attention turned from you? Am I correct? Did you have expectations, Miss Bennet? If so, you would have been sadly fooled to know Mr. Wickham had little to account for him beyond his easy manner. I am surprised he managed to find the coin to join the militia."

Mr. Darcy's tone had taken on the nature of a taunt, and Elizabeth took instant offense. "I would not say I was abandoned, sir," she hissed. "A gentleman has as much right to seek a fortune in the woman he marries as does a young lady in her choice of husbands."

"I am well aware of Mr. Wickham's constant need for funds," Mr. Darcy said sarcastically.

"Naturally, you would claim as such," she accused as she replaced the miniature on the table.

He advanced on her. "I suppose Mr. Wickham filled your pretty head with a litany of lies," he accused.

Elizabeth liked the idea that Mr. Darcy considered her to be pretty, but she would not permit him to speak to her, as if her opinions held no merit. "Your character, sir, was unfolded in a recital which I received from Mr. Wickham many years prior. In what imaginary act of friendship can you defend yourself? Who that knew of Mr. Wickham's misfortunes could not take an eager interest in the gentleman's concerns?"

"His misfortunes!" Mr. Darcy charged in contempt. "Yes, his misfortunes were great indeed, and I imagine they grew with each retelling."

They stood toe-to-toe. The breathing of each increased with their closeness. Elizabeth's argument died on her lips. Only the presence of this man before her held any merit.

She looked up into his eyes and viewed a world she would never know. At length, she ventured, "Are we arguing, Mr. Darcy? I would not wish to argue with you."

His hand rose slowly to caress her cheek gently with a brush of his fingertips. "I possess no wish to fight with you either, Miss Bennet, especially not over some tale you heard five years past from a man with no scruples."

She nodded her agreement before she asked, "Will you some day tell me the truth of Mr. Wickham's assertions?" The idea that she would never know what had truly occurred between Mr. Darcy and Mr. Wickham saddened her, for she truly wanted to hear the triumph of the gentleman standing before her. In another week, she would leave Mr. Darcy and this moment behind.

"There are so many things I wish to share with you." Mr. Darcy sounded as breathless as did she.

He was looking down upon her with such earnestness and a return of the tenderness she had viewed that day in the hallway outside of her quarters, that she did not know what to think. Elizabeth's insides turned to liquid, but, ironically, her throat had gone dry. For a long moment, neither of them moved. Then, as if some great force demanded their closeness, he yanked her into his embrace.

Instinctively, Elizabeth tilted her chin upward. Her heart pounded so hard she thought surely Mr. Darcy must be able to hear it. She knew he intended to kiss her, but she experienced no fear; rather, she felt safer in his embrace than she had since well before her father's passing. She recognized the same want coursing through her veins that had formed upon his features.

She waited in breathless anticipation for the kiss she knew Mr. Darcy was contemplating. But, suddenly, the warmth of his gaze dissipated and was replaced by contempt. Mr. Darcy stiffly released her and stepped back.

It took a few extra seconds before Elizabeth's mind cleared long enough to hear Colonel Fitzwilliam's voice as he spoke to someone who was evidently Mr. Nathan delivering the tea cart.

Mr. Darcy said through tight lips. "I sincerely apologize for my behavior, ma'am. I shan't permit another infringement on your person."

With that he crossed to sit behind his desk, assuming a position indicating nothing of importance had passed between them. Shakily, she sat in the nearest chair and prayed that the earth would open up and swallow her whole. She had likely ruined any chances of receiving a letter of character from the colonel's relations. How could they recommend her to another family when she had blatantly welcomed Mr. Darcy's kiss. "And to think," she murmured under her breath, "I am only at Pemberley because I refused another gentleman's attentions. Yet, who would believe me now?"

* * *

Thankfully, the Pemberley steward's wife had reported that her husband had been called out to address an issue on the far side of the estate; therefore, Elizabeth was not required to remain in Mr. Darcy's study very long. Although she was upset over her foolishness, she did not permit herself time to brood. Instead, she made her way to the nursery to enjoy a few minutes with the children. Odd as it would be to say the words aloud, the children had a calming effect on her composure. Likely, it was because she was expected to think upon another, rather than to dwell upon the disaster she had created. "My life," she whispered as she rocked Mr. Darcy's daughter to sleep while also overseeing the drawings that the Hurst boys made. "This is my future, and I must not ever forget my place again."

Although a little too boisterous for a nursery setting, the boys each possessed a sweet nature. All they required was a bit more attention and a steady hand. Elizabeth had briefly thought perhaps she could approach Mr. Hurst about joining the man's household, but she did not think she would be welcomed by either Mrs. Hurst or Miss

Bingley. Moreover, Philip Hurst had told her that his father had released their nurse and planned to hire a tutor for them after Christmastide. The boys said they were soon to leave for school, and, in truth, they would require more than she could provide them in that manner.

She knew others were to join the house party after Christmas, but she had begun to think it would be best for her to depart prior to that time. "Tomorrow," she whispered against the child's fluff of dark hair. "Tomorrow is Christmas, and all will be filled with good spirits." Tomorrow, she would ask for a private meeting with Lady Matlock and plead for some sort of recommendation. Elizabeth thought Mr. Darcy would not share what occurred between them with her ladyship, for, from what Elizabeth could determine, the gentleman was exactly that: A "gentleman." He would not speak of his part in what could have been an embarrassing situation for both of them. If they had been caught, they would have been made to marry or the family would have paid her to go away and keep quiet about the situation. "Or they may have driven me from Pemberley without even a farewell and a confirmation of Lady Newland's claims."

"Tomorrow," she repeated, setting her resolve.

"I am back," Mrs. Anderson announced. "You should return to your quarters and prepare for supper."

Elizabeth did not think she could tolerate an evening of Mr. Darcy ignoring her while paying attention to the other ladies, not that doing so appeared to be part of his nature. Yet, she was too embarrassed to face the man. Despite the foolhardiness of the situation, she knew she had desired the gentleman's kiss. Elizabeth wished heartily for a memory all her own, one that would last her for the remainder of her days.

"I told Hannah I would dine with you and the children this evening," she said without looking to the older woman. "Christmas is a time for friends and family. I would only be in their way, for I am neither."

* * *

She had been surprised when Colonel Fitzwilliam strolled into the nursery shortly after the supper hour had ended. "You were sorely missed this evening, my dear." He glanced to the nursery residents. "Why do you not walk with me in the gallery for a few minutes?"

Elizabeth thought perhaps he meant to present her with her "walking papers" and would prefer to do so without an audience.

"I would enjoy that, sir," she said, although pleasure was not in her repertoire, of late. Elizabeth accepted his arm and walked away with him.

Once they were from earshot of the nursery, he said. "My mother and the others remarked upon your absence this evening. I thought perhaps you and Darcy had exchanged words when I stepped from the study earlier today." Elizabeth attempted not to stiffen beside him or to pull away in denial. "You and Darcy appeared to be of one mind in discussing your suggestion, but when I returned, there was an evident coldness between you. As I am the one who is essentially sponsoring your presence in my cousin's household, I would like to know what occurred in my absence."

Elizabeth did not respond right away, rather, she took a moment to organize her thoughts. She decided she could tell the colonel of the confrontation over the miniature, but omit the heat coursing between her and Mr. Darcy afterwards.

"When I walked about the room, I came across the image of someone with whom I was very familiar," she explained.

The colonel's features screwed up in wonder. "An acquaintance you and Darcy have in common? Whoever could that be?"

She said softly, "Mr. Wickham."

"Wickham? That dastard!" The colonel paused at the end of the hall. "How could you have taken Wickham's acquaintance? I did not think you had ever traveled to Derbyshire. Pray, inform me of when you were permitted the man's company."

She braced her shoulders squarely before saying, "Mr. Wickham was attached to the local militia in Hertfordshire in 1813, as a lieutenant. As such, we were often in company at various entertainments." Elizabeth shrugged in embarrassment. "There was a time, many in the neighborhood thought Mr. Wickham had attached himself to me, but I was abandoned when Miss King came into an inheritance."

"You were blessed then," the colonel declared in sour tones. "The man was not worth the lead placed in his heart."

She asked, "Did not the late Mr. Darcy support Mr. Wickham at school?"

The colonel's frown lines deepened. "Wickham told you his tale of woe, did he?" He sighed heavily. "Did Darcy not explain what actually occurred?"

Elizabeth glanced away in remembrance. "Mr. Darcy and I exchanged a few heated words, but then we decided we would not argue over Mr. Wickham's character. I told your cousin I had heard Mr. Wickham's accusations, and, when your cousin was prepared to share it, I would willingly listen to Mr. Darcy's explanation."

The colonel did not respond immediately. "I can see how your knowledge of Mr. Wickham's version of the events that transpired between Wickham and Darcy would upset my cousin. Darcy is essentially a very private man and excessively proud of his family's name. You possess no idea how often Darcy paid off Wickham's debts simply because the jackanapes always made certain others knew of his slim connection to Pemberley and the Darcy name."

She said honestly, "Although I do not know the full of it, I cannot imagine the Mr. Darcy I have discovered at Pemberley can be the same man Mr. Wickham described. Even Miss Darcy has proved to be nothing of the nature of Mr. Wickham's description."

The colonel questioned, "Wickham spoke to you of Georgiana? What were you told of my cousins?"

"Of Mr. Darcy, Mr. Wickham claimed Pemberley's master can please where he chooses. It was said Mr. Darcy does not want abilities. He can be a quite conversable if he thinks doing so is worth his while. Among those who are at all his equals in consequence, he is a very different man from what he is to the less prosperous. That his pride never deserts him, but with the rich he is liberal-minded, just, sincere, rational, honorable, and, perhaps, agreeable, allowing for fortune and figure."

"Poppycock!" Displeasure continued to mark the colonel's features. "And of Miss Darcy?" he prompted.

"Mr. Wickham said he wished he could name Miss Darcy as amiable, but that she is too much like her brother—very, very proud.

He said, when she was a child, Miss Darcy was affectionate and pleasing and fond of him. The lieutenant went so far as to explain how he devoted hours and hours to her amusement, but he claimed Miss Darcy was nothing to him any longer. He went on to describe her as 'supposedly' highly accomplished."

"Is that all?" the colonel demanded.

"That was all Mr. Wickham said of Miss Darcy. There were a number of charges lodged against Mr. Darcy, but as Mr. Wickham is dead, there is no reason to worry over those details," Elizabeth assured. She paused before saying, "You are very fond of Miss Darcy and she of you."

"Most assuredly," the colonel declared. "Along with Darcy, I serve as one of Miss Darcy's guardians."

"And that is the extent of the affection between you, sir?" she asked with a lift of her brows.

"What else can there be?" he demanded.

"I have noticed the softness with which Miss Darcy looks upon you when she thinks no one is watching," she said with an easy smile.

"She has barely spoken to me since the day we took the sleighs out," he insisted.

"You mean since the day after you spent an evening by my side instead of hers," Elizabeth corrected.

A long pause ensued, before he said with a scowl, "To what you hint, cannot be."

Elizabeth offered no other suggestions. "As you say, sir. Just an observation. Do with the information as you see best." She dropped the subject completely, instead she asked the colonel of the possibility of Hannah's continued employment at Pemberley after Elizabeth was to leave. She did not mention her plans to depart as quickly as possible. However, if she must leave her new "friends" behind, Elizabeth wished to know they were all well-situated. She would prefer to think on them always as such. Everyone except her, that is. Even if she could claim another position, her heart would remain at Pemberley and in the hands of its master.

Chapter thirteen

Christmas Day, 1818

Darcy had been less than pleased with the fact that Miss Bennet had chosen not to join their party last evening for Christmas Eve services and to sit in the pews set aside for them. Instead, for the midnight services, she had stood beside her maid, as if she were a servant in his household. No one had asked of the lady's purpose, but Darcy knew they all had taken notice of her actions.

On this particular day, he had intentionally tarried in the morning room for the opportunity to speak to her, but the lady had reportedly taken her breakfast in the nursery with Mrs. Anderson and the children.

Later, after morning services, which she did not attend, Darcy had hoped she would join Mrs. Anderson and the children when they came down to spend a few minutes with the others in a private celebration of Christmas. He had smiled and played with Cassandra, presenting his daughter a tettering horse, much to the child's delight, but his eyes remained on the empty door, and his heart knew instant regret.

The countess presented each of the gentlemen a pen knife and each of the ladies a new scarf as part of their planned group Christmas celebration. Before the guests had come down, he, Georgiana, the colonel, and Lady Matlock had met in the countess's suite to exchange gifts of a more private nature.

He wanted to ask Fitzwilliam of the conversation his cousin had held with the lady last evening, but Darcy dared not to intrude after viewing the colonel's perplexed expression when he rejoined everyone in the drawing room. Darcy had wondered if perhaps the lady had told his cousin what had transpired between Darcy and her. He did not think she would purposely place a wedge between him and his favorite cousin; yet, how well did he truly know the woman?

After Darcy met with his staff to present each a token of his gratitude for their service, a cold supper was set out for him and his guests, and he excused his servants for an afternoon and evening off.

As the ladies took turns at the instrument, he and the others joined their voices to sing favorite hymns and other songs, but his heart was in another part of Pemberley.

When everyone returned to their rooms to dress for supper, he had known surprise when his cousin followed Darcy to his quarters.

"I wish to speak to you in private," the colonel said as they entered the bedroom together.

Darcy suspected Fitzwilliam's choice of topics would be Miss Bennet; therefore, he braced himself for his cousin's recriminations. "What is your pleasure?" he asked as he untied his cravat and tossed it on a nearby chair. His guilt was already choking him, he certainly did not require a tight-fitting cravat to finish the job.

"My recent conversation with Miss Bennet," Edward admitted.

Darcy poured them each a brandy. Handing one to his cousin, he said, "As I suspected."

The colonel explained, "The lady told me of how you two argued over Mr. Wickham."

Darcy sipped his brandy to stall his response. "Who would believe a complete stranger to me would also hold a connection to Mr. Wickham and would have heard many of the man's lies?"

"From what the lady shared, Wickham spoke often of both you and Georgiana," Fitzwilliam explained.

An alarm went off in Darcy's head. "Did Wickham tell her or the others in the village in Hertfordshire of his failed attempt to elope with Georgiana?"

"I do not think so, for I specifically asked her what Wickham had shared. I have the feeling she has heard of how your father sponsored Wickham at school and how you denied him the living at

Kympton, but the lady only said Wickham spoke of Georgiana being as prideful as you."

Darcy asked, "Do you think such is all Miss Bennet knows? When we exchanged words regarding Wickham's character, the lady spoke of my reducing Wickham to a state of penury, but she said nothing of Georgiana to me."

The colonel finished his brandy. "When you created that corner of your study as a tribute to your father, I disagreed with your keeping that demme miniature of Wickham. My disapproval has not slackened: Throw the demme piece of wood into the fire and use it for kindling. It can bring neither you nor Georgiana pleasure, and it sure as hell brings me none."

Darcy made no excuses. "You are correct." He paused to look off at something not there. "My father is likely as disappointed with me as he is of Wickham. He entrusted Georgiana's care to me, and I failed both him and my sister."

The colonel set his empty glass on a side table. "As I brought Miss Bennet into this house, with your permission, I wish to speak to Georgiana regarding what has occurred and provide her a gentle warning. From what Miss Bennet shared, I doubt the subject will ever come up, but it is best if we advise Georgiana of the slim possibility."

"Do you wish me to accompany you?" Darcy realized he should have already spoken to Georgiana about his encounter with Miss Bennet, but his mind had been too full of that particular lady and his desire to kiss her to see to his sister's comfort.

Fitzwilliam straightened the cut of his uniform. "If you do not mind, I would speak to her alone. I owe Georgiana an apology," his cousin declared.

"As do I," Darcy countered.

"Nevertheless," Fitzwilliam insisted, "I demand the pleasure. I will keep you informed and send for you if I am unable to calm Georgiana's fears." His cousin was nearly to the door when he paused again. "I almost forgot. Miss Bennet wondered if you might have a position available at Pemberley for her maid."

"Will the lady not require Hannah's services when she leaves Pemberley?"

The colonel shook off the idea. "When we departed Newland Hall, I could not permit Miss Bennet to travel alone with me and Captain Stewart. Doing so would only have proved Lady Newland's accusations correct. At the local posting inn, I meant to hire a maid for only a few days, but Hannah recognized me and begged to ride on top of Stewart's coach to Derbyshire, for she had been set to return to her father's house for Christmastide. I imagine now that she is in Derbyshire, she realizes she has no desire to return to Gloucestershire and her work in her uncle's inn."

Darcy admitted, "I would need to consult Mrs. Reynolds first. Yet, I still do not see how Miss Bennet will no longer require a maid when she departs Pemberley."

His cousin simply said, "The lady and I have a contract. Miss Bennet will hopefully have more than one choice to make after Twelfth Night."

* * *

Elizabeth had agreed to tend the children from the time Mr. Darcy pardoned his servants for the evening's festivities to the time they would all claim their beds. She had insisted that Mrs. Anderson should visit with her daughter and grandchildren on Christmas Day. What use did Elizabeth have for the day other than to spend it away from the man who had quite rightly bewitched her.

"You be certain, miss?" the woman asked a dozen times. With each asking, Elizabeth had assured the woman of her willingness to remain in the nursery. She would not admit, even to herself, that she was hiding away from Mr. Darcy, biding her time until she could leave Pemberley forever.

As she sat in the rocking chair, cooing sweet nothings to the man's daughter, Elizabeth permitted herself the tears she had held in check for more years than she could recall.

"It is my fault, little one," she said as she kissed the child's silky hair. "Your father holds none of the blame. It was all me. I permitted myself to be swept away by Mr. Darcy's kindness. I allowed myself a dream of a future. It has been so long since someone saw me as more than a governess. How could I not have responded to such a handsome man? How could I not be drawn to him?"

She caressed the sleeping child's cheek with the tip of her finger. "Someday, sweet child, you shall understand my response to the heat I witnessed in his eyes and the pure joy of being held in the protection of his arms.

"Unfortunately, I did not realize how quickly my feelings had become engaged, but, sadly, I will leave Pemberley soon." She smiled upon the child. "You shall be the fortunate one, for you shall always claim a place in your father's heart. I sincerely wish I could say the same; yet, nothing can occur between him and me. Mr. Darcy apologized for his behavior, but I cannot do the same, for, at this very moment, my dearest child, I still desire his kiss, and it breaks my heart to know, after tomorrow, I shall never set eyes upon the gentleman again."

* * *

Darcy had avoided making a second call upon the nursery when he learned Miss Bennet had permitted Mrs. Anderson time to visit with her grandchildren for Christmas Day. The gesture had been typical of the lady's behavior, but it frustrated him further because he knew he was the reason the woman avoided joining him and the others.

Their small party had enjoyed the wassail bowl, a cold supper, songs, and impromptu dancing, as well as the warmth of the Yule log and friends all about. Even so, Darcy recognized how the hole in his soul had grown larger. Before, when he attempted to convince himself he could live without affection, he might have been satisfied, but, since taking Miss Bennet's acquaintance, he felt the humdrum life he lived with Anne would be his destiny.

Depression had followed him about throughout the day. Each time someone entered the drawing room, he had looked up in hope of viewing Miss Bennet's fine countenance, only to know disappointment. He had spent the evening attempting to appear happy—had carried on superficial conversations to be polite—had smiled and nodded his approval, while being completely miserable.

His cousin had reported on Georgiana's initial concern with Miss Bennet's knowledge of Mr. Wickham, but, in Darcy's observation, he was, apparently, the only one constantly looking to the door for the "governess's" entrance.

Fitzwilliam and Georgiana spent the majority of the evening with their heads together, even going so far as to exchange a quick kiss under the kissing bough. Many kisses had been shared over the course of the evening, but Darcy had avoided the ball of mistletoe and evergreens as if it were the plague, even going so far as exiting through the servants' door when he returned to his quarters for fear that Miss Bingley lurked about the main hall waiting for him.

"I would have gladly kissed Miss Bennet," he admitted to his reflection in the mirror. "Yet again, a brief kiss might not have been enough to satisfy me. I did not wish for a kiss of friendship when I held the lady in my arms in my study. I wished to brand her as mine, instead of her being betrothed to Fitzwilliam.

"Like the lady, I wish I could lock myself away—hide the shame I feel for desiring a woman meant for my cousin. Thy shalt not covet—" he said as he turned to sit heavily in a nearby chair. "Without a doubt, Fitzwilliam will ask me to stand up with him, and, dearest God, how will I hold my silence when the vicar asks for objections?"

He buried his face in his hands. He accepted the blame for what nearly had occurred in his study, but, in his estimation, and Darcy had considered the moment enough times to hold an opinion, Miss Bennet desired his kiss equally as much as he had desired to kiss her. He had read the eagerness in her features—had heard the hitch in her breathing. Had Anne, even once, welcomed his touch? Darcy did not believe his late wife had ever responded to him with anything more than polite tolerance.

"I have been guarded in my interactions with every female I have encountered since I was sixteen. Then, why this reaction to this particular woman and why now? How could a man not be jealous of Fitzwilliam's good fortune in claiming Miss Bennet?"

He stood suddenly to pace the room, no longer having the ability for stillness. "Is it not ironic that I questioned the speed with which the colonel attached himself to the woman when I have known her less than a week? I should be asking what sorcery the lady practices and whether she purposely led Lieutenant Newland on, but I know she did not set her sights on me. I have experienced more than two dozen women who have all but crawled naked into my bed in order to entrap me. All Miss Bennet did was make herself useful to the household and to share my dreams for Pemberley. She wore no fine jewels, displayed no 'so-called' feminine attributes such as each woman in our company did this evening on the instrument, batted no long eyelashes at me, although I must admit I have never gazed into a finer set of eyes, the most compelling eyes I have ever beheld. A man could easily become lost in them."

He paused before the mirror again. "You cannot ill-use the woman. You must hold yourself in check. Another week and then she will be gone. When the weather permits, you will go to London and find a wife that better suits you." Even as he said the words aloud, Darcy thought the first part of his assertion achievable, but not the second.

* * *

Although she had told Mrs. Anderson to spend the night at her daughter's house, the woman had returned shortly after nine of the clock. Therefore, Elizabeth had returned to her quarters to prepare for her departure from Pemberley. Earlier in the day, she had written two letters—one to the countess to thank the lady for her kindness and one to the colonel offering similar sentiments. She knew she should also write to Mr. Darcy, but her heart ached too much with the simple idea of leaving him to place pen to paper.

She had decided not to approach Lady Matlock for a letter of character: Elizabeth would deal with whatever should come to pass with the incident with Lieutenant Newland. She would not impose upon Lady Matlock's goodness in that manner. She had reasoned that there were many wealthy merchants, such as Mr. Bingley, who would be seeking a governess for their daughters. Those of the middle class were, generally, simply happy to be employing a gentleman's daughter in their households.

"Good evening, Miss Bennet," Hannah said with a happy smile.

"Oh, Hannah, you appear quite polished in the Darcy livery." She scooped the girl into an embrace. "I am so happy you have claimed a position at Pemberley."

"It be all unexpected," the girl said as she spun in place to show off the livery provided to Mr. Darcy's servants. "Mrs. Reynolds be callin' me into her quarters and she offers me a position."

"What type of maid will you be?" Elizabeth asked as she tugged the girl closer to the bed so they might sit together.

"Don't be knowin' for certain, but it not be in the kitchen. Even so, the work can't be harder than what I did in Gloucestershire. At my uncle's inn, I be expected to do it all—clean and cook and serve. For now, I am to do what I've been doin': tendin' to you and assistin' where needed."

Elizabeth tightened her hold on Hannah's hand. "Then, after tomorrow, you must negotiate with Mrs. Reynolds regarding your permanent assignment at Pemberley."

"What mean you?" Hannah asked in concern. "I thought you'd be at Pemberley until after Twelfth Night."

Fighting back the tears rushing to her eyes, Elizabeth said softly, "I must be in London if I am to secure a new position."

"Did Lady Matlock provide you a character?" Hannah questioned.

Elizabeth admitted, "I did not ask for one." She placed a smile upon her lips. "I will walk into the village tomorrow and claim a seat on the mail coach when it arrives in Lambton. I understand it arrives after six of the evening. The letters on the vanity will make my explanations to her ladyship and Colonel Fitzwilliam."

Hannah declared, "I'll go with you. It's too dangerous fer ye to be on the road alone."

"Only last week, you thought to walk into the village alone," Elizabeth protested.

"I not be carryin' me portmanteau, and, moreover, I knows the road. You do not," Hannah countered. "Besides, Mrs. Reynolds' be sayin' I'm to serve you first. Permittin' you to walk into the village alone wouldn't be doin' what I be hired to do."

Elizabeth wished to argue further, but she did not have the heart to do so. "You are so good to me, Hannah."

"When will you leave?" Hannah asked.

Elizabeth sucked in a deep breath to steady her resolve. "About half past ten," she explained.

"After the master and the others leave to deliver baskets to his cottagers for St. Stephen's Day," Hannah quickly deduced. "Oh, miss, I thought you be made of sterner stuff."

Elizabeth reluctantly said, "Not as much as I would like, I fear."

Hannah's arms instantly came about her, and Elizabeth permitted the maid to provide her a few moments of self-pity. Tomorrow would call for her strength again, but, this evening, Elizabeth would claim the kindness of the only friend she had had since the day she walked away from her uncle's home in London to become a governess.

Chapter fourteen

Saturday, 26 December 1818

The guests had gathered in the main hall to be a part of Pemberley's annual St. Stephen's Day activities. Pemberley's celebration was a tradition going back several generations and one Darcy enjoyed for its simplicity. Outside the main door of Pemberley House were wagons loaded with baskets of food and small kegs of beer to be delivered to each of his cottagers' households, where he and his party would be welcomed by the families within.

As he looked on, his guests bundled up for the cold, donning coats and gloves and scarfs and shawls, although Darcy thought it too "warm" for the snow of which many of them spoke. Plans were forming for another sleigh ride beyond the one before them to deliver the presentations to his tenants. The Pemberley party hoped for another day in the snowy hills together.

Laughter filled the hall as servants scrambled to fetch muffs and scarfs; yet, Darcy knew no real pleasure in the assemblage, for, once more, Miss Bennet had sent her regrets. As foolish as it would sound to say the words aloud, he wanted her opinion of the festivities—to learn how the lady viewed the activity, which suddenly felt more antiquated than he initially thought.

He caught his cousin's arm for a brief exchange. "Have you spoken to Miss Bennet? I have not seen the lady since she departed my study three days prior. I thought she might enjoy knowing I have spoken to Mr. Stanley, and my steward believes several small 'businesses,' of the sorts she suggested could be brought to Pemberley's doors."

Fitzwilliam shrugged off the question. "Beyond my conversation with her where we spoke of Wickham, I have not encountered Miss Bennet."

Darcy knew he frowned, but he could not conceal his displeasure. "Should you not be more concerned regarding how Miss Bennet has essentially withdrawn from company?"

"Would you have me compel her to go against her will?" the colonel demanded.

"Most assuredly, I would not," Darcy said through tight lips. "Neither would I have a guest in my house be ignored and treated as a servant."

The colonel said, "Then, when we return to the house, perhaps you should speak to the lady personally regarding what is expected of those who visit Pemberley."

Darcy swallowed his retort, instead asking, "May I count on you to organize those on the second sleigh? I can take the countess up with me, if you would agree to squire Georgiana. I prefer the family sits at the head of each of the sleighs."

His cousin nodded sharply. "As you wish." Fitzwilliam started away, but he paused to say, "If you hold no objections, I would speak to you privately when we all return to the house."

Darcy attempted not to react with concern. He thought his cousin was likely aware of Darcy's interest in Miss Bennet and meant to put an end to it. "As you wish."

* * *

The day had not gone as Darcy had hoped. They were only halfway through their stops when the cold rain began, and he had sent everyone back to Pemberley House, charging the colonel and Bingley with the task of seeing that everyone arrived safely and were provided hot tea and brandy as needed.

He was not so fortunate, as, several hours later, Darcy personally delivered the last of the baskets to the farthest set-back home farm on the estate.

"Mr. Darcy, I didnae expect to view you, what with the weather bein' what it is," Mr. Ahrens declared.

Darcy attempted to disguise the shiver claiming his spine, but he knew he had failed. "I shan't keep you, Ahrens. Just a gesture of my continued gratitude." Mr. Farrin handed over the last of the items. "Good day, sir."

Darcy returned to the wagon. "Take us home, Farrin," he told his driver.

"Be glad for both of us to know a hot bath, sir."

"Amen to that idea." Darcy glanced around to note how the cold rain had turned the snow-covered ground into an icy expanse. Trees hung low as the temperature dropped, and the rain created long icicles off the evergreen branches. There would be no sleigh ride today, after all, for the Pemberley party.

"How long, Mr. Farrin?" he asked.

"With these conditions, I imagine thirty to forty minutes, sir."

Darcy shivered again. "Care before speed, Farrin. I do not wish for us to be tipped over and need to walk home."

* * *

Elizabeth had waited for a half hour to pass after the departure of the sleighs before she followed Hannah down the servants' stairs to the main floor, where they escaped through a door to a balcony leading down to a stretch of land backing up to the woods and the main entrance of Pemberley. Elizabeth had insisted upon carrying her own portmanteau, but she was soon regretting the choice as the trunk became heavier and heavier as she side-stepped roots and downed limbs before reaching the main road leading away from Pemberley.

She had left behind two of the gowns Mr. Darcy had presented her. It did not feel proper for her to take the gowns when she had not earned them. Therefore, she had only brought the green one she had worn on that delightful evening five days earlier. Elizabeth had claimed there was no room in her portmanteau for the other gowns, but she was worried someone at Pemberley would take it on himself or herself to claim she had stolen them. She supposed those staying at the house could say the same about the moss-colored dress; yet, she felt assured Mr. Darcy would not pursue her for a crime, for she had served the gentleman's household while she was in residence.

Within three quarters of an hour, she and Hannah stepped out on the road to Lambton. "How far?" she asked the maid as she shifted the portmanteau in her grasp.

"Five miles, miss." Hannah responded. "Be you certain you do not wish to return to the manor house?"

Elizabeth shook off the idea. "When I lived in Hertfordshire, I was considered to be an excellent walker."

Hannah's eyebrow rose in challenge. "Nothin' of ill meanin', but that be five years ago." She shook her head, half in amusement and half in disapproval. "I'll take the large bag until you catch your breath. You take the smaller one."

They had walked nearly two miles, often switching out the bags they carried, when a man, dressed in the manner of a farmer, with a donkey cart overtook them. "Miss Hannah, be that you?" the man asked as he stopped his progress.

Hannah paused to look to the man. "Mr. Norton, how good to view a friendly face."

"I thought you be someplace in the south," the man declared with a wide smile that was missing several teeth.

"I was, sir, but Miss Bennet here gives me a position as her maid so I cud visit with me family for Christmastide."

"Don't appare you be visitin' right now."

"No, sir. Miss Bennet means to catch the mail coach this evenin'. I took a position at Pemberley and will return there after I sees the lady off."

The man gestured to the empty cart. "Climb in, and I'll see ye into the village. I've finished all me deliveries for today and glad of it."

Hannah quickly and efficiently lifted the portmanteau onto the back of the cart without asking Elizabeth if she would agree to accept the man's offer. Following Hannah's example, Elizabeth set the smaller bag on the cart and climbed up into the small space to huddle closer to Hannah. She suddenly realized how much the temperature had dropped.

"We thank you kindly, sir," she dutifully repeated.

"Save yer thanks, miss. If'n ye be a friend to Miss Hannah, ye be a friend of mine. The Crownleys be good people."

As the man set the donkey in motion again, Hannah asked, "To whom did you deliver supplies today?"

"The Craigs over on t'other side of Pemberley," the man explained, talking over his shoulder so they could hear. "Already a cold rain there, makin' it hard to keep one's footin'. Glad the donkey is more sure-footed than me. Likely have an icy way to go before mornin'."

Elizabeth asked, "Will the mail coach arrive?" She had not anticipated bad weather.

"Doubt it, miss. The coach be comin' from the west. Likely already iced in. Lambton and Pemberley be the same by this time tomorrow."

Elizabeth looked to Hannah for guidance. "Do not worry. If the mail coach cannot reach Lambton tonight, then those at Pemberley will also be required to hunker down. We'll stay at the inn with my parents."

"But you shall lose your position by not returning to Pemberley this evening." She looked around frantically. "Leave me now," Elizabeth rushed to say. "Hurry back to Pemberley. Mr. Norton will see me into the village, will you not, sir?"

Hannah's scowl deepened. "I agreed to stay with you until you leave Pemberley. I keep me word, miss."

* * *

Nearly five hours after he set out for his rounds this morning, Darcy reentered Pemberley, cold and exhausted, but with a feeling of satisfaction: He had personally carried on his family's tradition, and he thought his parents would be extremely proud of him. Odd as it would be to say the words aloud, he wished to rush to Miss Bennet's room and permit the lady to speak the words he knew Lady Anne Darcy would have done at this moment.

"Very pleased to have you home, sir," Mr. Nathan said as he assisted Darcy in removing his overcoat, which was heavy and dripping water from the rain.

"Glad to be within these walls, at last. Did everyone else return unscathed?"

"Yes, sir. I believe everyone is in his or her rooms preparing for supper."

Darcy nodded his understanding. "I need to be out of these wet clothes and soon. Send for Sheffield and have Murray bring up water for a hot bath. Also, ask Cook to have a maid bring me some bread and cheese. I missed the midday meal."

"Right away, sir."

Darcy took the stairs two at a time and within a quarter hour, he was enjoying a bath in a tub of hot water.

"I have your clothes laid out, sir," Sheffield said as he held a large towel for Darcy's use. "We were all quite concerned, sir." Darcy knew his servants fretted over his safety. After all, he had yet to produce an heir for Pemberley, which would essentially secure their futures, as well as his. "I have set the plate with the bread and cheese on the small table beside your bed."

Darcy nodded his acceptance as his man began to dress him, providing Darcy his small clothes, breeches, and shirt. "How long until supper?" he asked, not having looked at the clock all afternoon.

"About an hour and a half, sir. Should I ask Cook to hold the meal?"

"No, that is enough time. I plan to sit before the fire and warm myself before I dress for supper. Return in about three-quarters of an hour."

"Very good, sir." The valet disappeared from the room.

Darcy had just leaned back in his chair and closed his eyes when a soft knock rattled his quiet time. "Come," he called.

His cousin's voice asked, "Do you still have time to speak to me?"

All Darcy wanted to do was to claim a short nap, but he knew he must settle things with Fitzwilliam and soon. "Yes, please come in." When his cousin was settled across from him, Darcy said, "I suppose you've come to speak to me regarding Miss Bennet."

The colonel looked upon him as if Darcy had been knocked sideways by a great blow. "And why would I wish to speak to you regarding Miss Bennet?"

"Have you truly no care for a woman you specifically brought to Pemberley to take the acquaintance of your family?" Darcy accused.

Fitzwilliam countered, "I promised Miss Bennet a holiday, not my undivided attention."

Darcy was on his feet immediately. "What do you mean you promised Miss Bennet a holiday? Do you consider your offer of marriage nothing more than a holiday?"

Fitzwilliam was on his feet also. "What bird-brained idea is this? I have not offered my hand to any lady, that is, unless you object to my courting your sister."

It took Darcy a few extra seconds to comprehend what his cousin said. "You wish to court Georgiana?"

"Is that not what I just said?" the colonel asked with a lift of his eyebrows in challenge. "I know after your marriage to Anne, you are skeptical about the wisdom of solidifying blood lines by marriages within a family, but this great nation's history has multiple examples of such marriages, and they were successful."

"I know our country's history as well as you," Darcy declared. "Georgiana?" he asked. "You have served as her guardian. Can you separate those feelings of protection from the emotions necessary to take her in marriage? I have always said I would not permit my sister to marry a man she did not affect or one who did not affect her. I wish my sister to be accepted for more than her dowry."

Fitzwilliam paused before answering. "I have asked myself those questions also, such is the reason I am before you now pleading for an 'informal' courtship without the mention of marriage until Georgiana and I have time to decide whether we will suit or not. I mean to leave the army by summer and ask father for my inheritance."

Darcy said, "I think you will find Georgiana agreeable, and as she will soon reach her majority, I may have no say in her choice of husbands."

"You believe Georgiana favors me?" the colonel asked. He appeared to be dumbfounded by the possibility. "Miss Bennet said something similar, but I was not certain whether to believe her or not."

It was Darcy's turn to bewildered. "What will you do with Miss Bennet if you mean to court Georgiana?"

"Are we back to Miss Bennet again?" the colonel accused. "If you are so worried for the lady, then I give over my allegiance to the woman to you."

145

"I cannot care for Miss Bennet," Darcy hissed, "for she is your betrothed."

"My what?" Fitzwilliam appeared flabbergasted by Darcy's assumption. "I am not betrothed to Miss Bennet or any woman, for that matter. Whatever gave you such an idea?"

Darcy crossed to the desk and retrieved his cousin's note announcing his arrival. "Read this and tell me you were not declaring yourself betrothed to Miss Bennet."

Fitzwilliam snatched the note from Darcy's fingers to read his own words. A long silence followed before the colonel said, "I certainly did not mean to imply what you assumed. I just thought once you and mother took the lady's acquaintance that one of you would provide her a letter of character to counteract Lady Newland's venom."

"You claimed to hold an 'understanding' with the woman," Darcy accused. "Customarily, that particular word is used to indicate a marriage proposal. In addition, Miss Bennet referred to your arrangement as a 'contract.'"

"I most assuredly comprehend how all this appeared," his cousin repeated in placating tones, "yet, I do not quite see how this is such a monumental endeavor. Both Miss Bennet and I understood the terms of our 'contract.' It was you—"

"And the countess," Darcy added.

"Dear God, are you saying my mother also thought I was engaged to Miss Bennet?" his cousin demanded.

"Your express was addressed to both her ladyship and me," Darcy countered. "Naturally, I shared it with my aunt."

The colonel sighed heavily. "And Georgiana? Does she know of this supposed proposal also?"

Darcy shrugged. "I warned my sister not to place her hopes on a man who had pledged himself to another."

Fitzwilliam started for the door. "I have explanations to make to the two most important women in my life. You will pardon my hasty exit. I fear I may no longer require your permission to marry Georgiana. After my confession, your sister may refuse my suggestion of an 'informal' courtship until she reaches her majority."

The colonel was out the door before Darcy could comprehend what had just occurred. He stood staring at the closed door for the longest time, digesting his conversation with his cousin. "The lady is not betrothed to Fitzwilliam," he whispered to the empty room. "Is there a chance?"

His breath caught in his throat. Instinctively, he rubbed a spot in the center of his chest where the ache in his heart had opened up again: He had come so close to kissing her, and then he shoved her away. Would she forgive him? Would she understand? Would she ignore how foolish he had acted?

Darcy had to know immediately. "Demme, the supper bell," he growled when he heard the first warning ring below. He sat quickly and began pulling on his stockings, but stopped when he realized Miss Bennet might ignore the supper bell again this evening. "She has withdrawn from the others, and I cannot have her do so this time." He rushed to pull the bell cord before grabbing a pair of boots from where they were lined up in the dressing room.

Within minutes, Sheffield appeared in the room. Viewing Darcy tugging at his boots, he said, "Permit me, sir."

"No!" Darcy waved off the valet. "I must speak to Mrs. Reynolds immediately. Fetch her here, Sheffield."

With an odd grin, his valet rushed away to do Darcy's bidding, and he finally managed to don the polished brown leather boots. He tucked his shirt inside his breeches and buttoned his waistcoat before Sheffield returned with the housekeeper in tow.

"You sent for me, Mr. Darcy," Mrs. Reynolds asked.

"Yes, I wish you to go to Miss Bennet's quarters and ask the lady to join me in my study before supper."

Sheffield held Darcy's jacket while Darcy watched Mrs. Reynolds's expression soften.

"I cannot, sir," she began. "Miss Bennet is not in her rooms."

Irritated, Darcy said, "Then find her wherever she is and tell the lady I must speak to her before the supper hour. Is she in the nursery?"

Mrs. Reynolds looked on him with true interest, which unnerved Darcy for a brief moment. At length, she said, "The young lady has left Pemberley. She took her belongings and walked into

147

Lambton. I permitted Hannah to go with her to make certain the young lady reached the village."

"When?" he demanded.

"I do not know for certain, sir, but sometime after everyone left this morning." She reached in her apron pocket to retrieve two letters, which she handed to him. "Miss Bennet left these, sir."

Darcy glanced to the names on the letters. "To my cousin and her ladyship," he murmured in disappointment. His knees giving out before he sat on the chair arm.

"To the people the young lady could speak her farewells, Master William," Mrs. Reynolds said softly.

"I do not understand." Darcy continued to stare at Miss Bennet's handwriting on the letters.

"The lady's heart did not wish to leave you," his housekeeper contended. "She could not rightly say 'farewell' to her affection for you."

Darcy looked up in surprise. "How can you be so certain?"

"Oh, Master, we all have stood in audience to how quickly the lady stole your heart. Mr. Nathan and I agreed we had never viewed you so engrossed in anyone as you were when you escorted the lady into Pemberley House that first day. For all you cared, everyone else gathered within could have gone to the Devil."

"But Miss Bennet does not—"

"Hannah says otherwise, sir," Sheffield disclosed from somewhere behind him.

"I ask again, are you two confident in your opinions?" he pleaded.

"Hannah was to prevent Miss Bennet's departure on the mail coach," Mrs. Reynolds explained. "We all hoped you would come to your senses when you learned of Miss Bennet's leave-taking."

Sheffield said softly, "The icy rain may have done the trick instead."

Finally remembering the cold rain, Darcy turned to look to the window. "The storm arrived early. Do you think she and Hannah made it into Lambton safely?"

Mrs. Reynolds motioned Sheffield to continue dressing Darcy. "I suppose you must discover that fact for yourself, sir."

Darcy scowled. "Are you managing my life, Mrs. Reynolds? I am no longer a child without a mother."

"I am not," she declared with a smile, "but, if I were, I would argue that you are a grown man who deserves a bit of happiness. I know no finer gentleman in all of England; yet, you will never reach your true greatness if you do not go after the woman you affect."

"My guests," he protested weakly as he retrieved his money clip, a Queen Anne revolver, and dry gloves.

"Will enjoy Cook's dishes even if you are not at the table," Sheffield declared. "Now, I am ordering your favorite horse to be saddled. A carriage would run off the road in these conditions, but Diablo is sure-footed enough if you take it slow."

"How am I to thank you properly?" he asked as he claimed several handkerchiefs from a drawer.

Mrs. Reynolds grinned widely. "Permit me to inform Miss Bingley that you intend to propose to Pemberley's own Christmas governess, Miss Bennet."

Chapter fifteen

Elizabeth carried several bowls of stew to a table near the door. Mr. Crownley had been happy to view both Hannah and her, not asking for an explanation of their sudden appearance in the village, all of which Elizabeth found quite peculiar, but, in reality, she knew very little of Hannah's life before meeting the girl in Gloucestershire, which was odd also, for Hannah had been employed by her uncle there. Why had the girl not stayed with her parents in Derbyshire? Yet, what was Elizabeth to say about how families functioned? Hers had been "peculiar" also. Elizabeth had said that she meant to catch the mail coach that would arrive at six. Nothing else had been discussed, and no questions had been asked.

"I've me doubts the coach'll arrive, but I could use your assistance while you wait."

"Most assuredly, I'd be happy to be of assistance," she had declared.

"Hannah'll show you what to do," he said and quickly disappeared into the kitchen.

That had been two hours earlier, and the inn had progressively become more and more crowded.

"I cannot believe anyone would purposely venture out on such a night," Elizabeth had said to Hannah on multiple occasions, but each time her friend had simply shrugged her response and continued to serve new customers.

A half-dozen travelers passing through the area had claimed rooms at the Rose and Crown, which was named after the man's wife "Rose" and a shortened version of his "surname." Mr. Crownley openly expressed his concern for a lack of rooms if the weather continued to be a sheet of ice coating all the surfaces. He, too, had commented on the nearly two dozen locals who had chosen to have their supper at the inn, but, again, Elizabeth did not know whether this was normal or not. The neighborhood in which she resided in Hertfordshire rarely had snow or ice storms, and, if they did, she was not certain what those in Meryton did when bad weather arrived, for she and her sisters would have been hunkered down at Longbourn, not on the road.

She had just set the last of the bowls of stew and a small loaf of dark bread on the table for a party of four when she heard a door to the outside open behind her, and, oddly, the busy room went instantly quiet. All eyes were turned toward the entrance, and so, she slowly rotated about to view what or, should she say, who had commanded such reverence as to hold the attention of all in attendance.

"Mr. Darcy," she murmured and reached out a hand to the back of a chair to steady her shakey curtsey, for her legs suddenly felt weak in the knees. He was a magnificent figure of a man, even though his coat dripped from the icy rain.

"Miss Bennet," he said with a bow, his voice ringing clearly off the wooden walls in the perfectly silent room.

Elizabeth noted Hannah quickly eased the door behind the gentleman closed. No one else stirred. All eyes were fixed on this poorly played tableau performed by the gentleman and her. "I did not expect you, sir," she managed to say.

"You spoke your farewells to the countess and my cousin, but you left no such closing for me."

Elizabeth noticed how he refused to look to the left or the right. She quickly realized he was as miserable as she with how this reunion was playing out in public. Therefore, she took a leap of faith and said what she prayed he wished to hear. "It was not in my power to say those words to you."

He closed his eyes briefly and sucked in a quick breath in what appeared to be relief. "That is excellent news, Miss Bennet."

"Would you not prefer to warm yourself by the fire, sir?" She gestured toward a chair placed nearby.

"Not until he proposes to you first," a man in the corner called out.

Elizabeth turned sharply to view Mr. Norton and another man she did not recognize. "There is no need—" she began, but Norton stood quickly.

"Although Crownley serves both a mighty fine stew and a corn chowder, we've all been waitin' for hours to hear Mr. Darcy's proposal, and we're not leavin' until we hears him speak the words. Crownley promised us a betrothal this evening. Why else be we out on a night not fit for a dog?"

All eyes turned to where Crownley stood at the open kitchen door, but Elizabeth concentrated on Hannah. "You told everyone to expect a proposal?" She found herself blushing as she looked once again to the gentleman. "I knew nothing of this, sir, and I apologize if you have been brought here on false pretenses." Her grip on the back of the chair tightened.

Mr. Darcy's lips broke into a spectacular smile. "You have no idea the number of false pretenses we have encountered in the last week, my dear." He briefly glanced to Hannah. "I suspect your maid took her orders from my housekeeper and butler. It was their and Mr. Sheffield's belief that your heart was as equally engaged as is mine. Were they correct?"

Elizabeth swallowed hard. From behind Mr. Darcy, Hannah ordered, "Tell the master the truth."

Briefly unable to form the words, Elizabeth nodded her answer. "You have my heart, sir," she said through the tears misting her eyes.

Mr. Darcy took several steps closer, coming to stand before her and claiming her hand from the back of the chair. "I do not wish to disappoint all who orchestrated this evening, and such is not my reason for following you to the village. I could do nothing less, for you have my heart, as well. Miss Elizabeth Bennet, would you do me the great honor of becoming my wife?"

She knew the tears rolled down her cheeks, but for the first time in forever, they were happy tears. Attempting to ignore the audience that watched her reactions, she said, "I can think of nothing grander. My answer is 'yes.'"

He was kissing her then. The room behind them filled with cheers, but all Elizabeth felt was the warmth of his lips and the dampness of both her cheeks and his coat. She would have liked to remain in his arms, but Hannah interrupted them to catch Elizabeth up in a hug while more than one of Mr. Crownley's customers shook Mr. Darcy's hand.

Elizabeth heard Mr. Crownley say, "The vicar is in attendance tonight if'n you wish to purchase a license, sir. My Hannah seems to think it would be appropriate to introduce your new wife to all of Derbyshire at your New Year's ball."

* * *

Darcy looked to where Hannah embraced Miss Bennet. "Ask the vicar to remain a bit longer," he told Crownley. "For now, provide everyone with a drink on my account while I speak to my betrothed in private regarding her wishes." He glanced about. "Is there a room we might use to discuss our future?"

Mr. Crownley gestured to the back of the inn. "Hannah's room is at the end of the hall."

"Miss Bennet," he said in false calmness, for around him everyone was laughing and cheering and talking over each other in celebration. "Might we discuss how we wish to proceed? Mr. Crownley says there is a small room we might use."

She appeared frightened and uncertain, but she nodded her agreement and accepted his outstretched hand. As they walked away, Crownley called out, "Drinks on Mr. Darcy."

They did not speak until he lit a candle and closed the door to block out the scene in the inn's dining area.

Before he had time to organize his thoughts, the lady said, "I shall not hold you to your proposal if you do not wish it, sir. Tell the others you learned of Lady Newland's accusations, and I chose to release you from your promise."

"About those accusations," he said ignoring her evident misery, "you and Fitzwilliam would have saved both of us the torment of the past I currently view upon your features, if you two had not led me and the countess to believe you were betrothed to my cousin."

She looked upon him as if he had grown another head. "When did I say the colonel and I were betrothed?" she demanded.

154

He stepped closer. He enjoyed having the upper hand with her. Darcy suspected there would be more than a few incidents of heated words passing between them over the next thirty or forty years, and he was looking forward to both the confrontations and the right to kiss her into submission, or be kissed into submission, for that matter. He had never felt so alive in his life. "You did not say you were betrothed to Fitzwilliam, but you did speak of a 'contract,' and my cousin spoke of an 'understanding' between you."

She opened her mouth to protest, but quickly snapped it shut. "The colonel suggested that the countess might provide me a letter of character to counteract Lady Newland's lack of recommendation."

"So my cousin has explained," he said with a smile. "Therefore, my urgency in reaching you before you departed Derbyshire."

She studied his features for an elongated moment. "Then your proposal was sincere?"

He smiled easily. "I might have preferred a more private moment with you, but my word is my bond," he said as he reached for her. "Now, you may kiss me again. I do not believe one kiss will sufficiently keep me entertained until I make you my wife."

He did not bother to wait for a response. Darcy could not explain why he wished to provoke her in this manner. Likely it was the lust that had haunted him since the moment he had sought her out in Pemberley's drive. Or, mayhap, it was that damnable voice in his head that said, *She is the one!* The heat between them increased to an almost unbearable point as he gathered her loosely into his embrace.

In that moment, Darcy knew Mrs. Reynolds was correct: He would never have known happiness without this woman in his life—no matter her penury, she was destined to be the mother of his children.

He had wanted her from the instant he had laid eyes on her. Unable to wait another second, Darcy lowered his head and took her mouth, not in the manner of the chaste kiss they had shared earlier, but one of sheer demand. A spark instantly flared to life when their lips met. It set him afire, as if their souls had melded together, connecting them from head to toe.

155

Desire crashed down on him, and it took every ounce of his renowned self-control not to carry her to Hannah's small bed and settle things between them here and now. He did not want to stop, but he made himself ease her from his embrace.

Her breathing was as heavy as his, which privately pleased him greatly: They would do well together.

"We have . . . some decisions . . . to make, and I do not think . . . Crownley will . . . provide us . . . privacy forever," he managed to say.

She looked upon him with such wonderment that he was half-tempted to finish what he had started. "What decisions?" she whispered on a breathy exhale.

Darcy could not prevent his smile. He would know many happy days ahead of him. "First," he began, "do you wish a long courtship?"

Her adorable face screwed up in concentration. "I should say I would prefer to wait, but—"

"But?" he asked, his heart lurching to a halt.

She patted his chest, as if she knew she must start his breathing again. "None of your second-guessing, Mr. Darcy," she ordered. "For a moment, I thought I would love to have my dear family with me, 'but' I realized you are all the family I require on my wedding day."

"You say the most delightful things, Miss Bennet."

He brought her into his arms again and simply held her. "Mr. Crownley has informed me that the vicar is among his patrons this evening," he suggested.

"And?" she questioned. The heat of her mouth penetrated the dampness of his fine lawn shirt. "But, we have no special license," she announced, "so there is no possibility of a marriage this evening."

"You are correct. And it is too far to ride to Doctors' Commons to beg for a special license from my godfather."

She shoved against his chest to escape. "The Archbishop of Canterbury is your godfather?" she asked in tones of disbelief.

Darcy grinned. "Did I forget to mention my family's roots can be traced to the Norman Conquest?"

"Do not attempt to bam me, Mr. Darcy. My courage always rises at every attempt to intimidate me."

Darcy continued to smile. "I am counting on it, love."

"Love?" she asked in a return of her qualms. "You love me?"

Darcy paused before responding. "I am obsessed with you. Desire you. Am miserable when you are not around. Can barely keep my hands off you. I do not know the definition of love; yet I suspect I love you, Elizabeth Bennet."

"Like you, sir, all I know of love is found in the books I have read, but if a deep fierce loyalty to another is a sign of love . . . if love means one's own sense of self grows through a relationship with another . . . if love means a real sense of pride in knowing another is successful . . . if love is a feeling of rightness and certainty, with an absence of doubt, then I love you, William."

Darcy reached for her again. The sound of his name on her lips was nearly his undoing. He caressed her cheek. "Then as neither of us appears to have an objection, I will accept Mr. Crownley's suggestion and have Mr. Brownstone join us in here. If I purchase the license today, we may marry in five—on the eve of the new year."

"On the day of your annual ball?" she asked breathlessly, reality obviously arriving.

"Or the day after or any day in the next few weeks. Just do not make me wait long, Elizabeth, for I am not a patient man by nature."

She glanced to the closed door. "It would seem that the village, which depends on Pemberley, is set upon seeing you take a wife."

"They seem to think we should begin our new life together on the eve of a new beginning," he added.

"I am agreeable," she said. "Do you hold objections?"

"I do not, love." He kissed her then, sealing their agreement.

* * *

Tuesday, 29 December 1818

It was another two days before they returned to Pemberley. The storm had taken down several trees that blocked the road between Lambton and the estate. Therefore, it was early on the morning of the twenty-ninth that a carriage occupied by the colonel and Bingley arrived at the inn. In many ways, Darcy regretted that they had come searching for him. He was quite happy to spend his days with Elizabeth, learning more of her life and discovering her unlimited smiles and kindness and intelligence, as well as the promise of passion in his marriage.

"I told you Darcy had not followed Miss Bennet to London, Bingley," his cousin announced as the pair entered the inn's common room.

Darcy and Elizabeth were enjoying tea together at "their" table in the inn's supper room. He and she had spent countless hours, with their heads together, and in full view of the inn's various patrons, yet, in a very private courtship.

Darcy stood to greet his cousin and Bingley, and he did not contradict Fitzwilliam's pronouncement, although Darcy knew he had been prepared to give pursuit if Miss Bennet had departed Lambton before he arrived. "I see the roads are finally open," he said as he shook each man's hand. In truth, Darcy would have been just as happy to remain from the reach of those at Pemberley. He did not want to share Elizabeth with others.

"The countess has had half your staff out assessing the damage, clearing roads, and making repairs," Bingley explained. His friend glanced to Elizabeth. "And how have you employed your time, Darcy?"

Darcy reached for Elizabeth's hand to assist her to stand beside him. "I have used these extra days splendidly, getting to know more of my betrothed."

Bingley grinned widely. "We were all wondering if such was so. Please accept my congratulations." His friend looked to the colonel. "We suspect your cousin will soon be making his own announcement."

Fitzwilliam said in what sounded of irritation, "I have my duty to the Army to consider before any such decisions are made."

Darcy wondered what had occurred in his absence, but he would learn the right of it soon enough. "Let us sit." He motioned to the extra chairs nearby. "I pray all is well at Pemberley."

Fitzwilliam said with a shrug, "With the countess, Mr. Nathan, and Mrs. Reynolds in charge, you have nothing of which to know concern."

Realizing his cousin was acting from sorts, Darcy motioned to Mr. Crownley to bring over fresh tea. Elizabeth must have noticed it also. "Permit me to assist Mr. Crownley for a few minutes. I shall bring over a plate of those cakes you enjoy, William."

All three men stood for her exit, but when they were settled again, his cousin asked, "When did you decide to extend your hand to Miss Bennet? Georgiana says you spoke of your admiration for the woman, but I did not realize you affected her. Please say this is not you acting in honor to save the family name. I promise you Miss Bennet never considered our agreement more than my extending a hand to a woman who was ill-used by one of my junior officers."

Darcy eyed his cousin with a bit of pity. "When did you become so self-centered, Fitzwilliam? If you had removed your nose from your own posterior, you might have noticed my sister's misery when she thought you favored Miss Bennet, as well as my obsession with Elizabeth. I only avoided Miss Bennet because I thought you two had an understanding. Others noticed. My staff and Miss Bennet's maid took notice and did what they could to bring us together. Even Miss Bingley noticed, for she attempted to dissuade my interests, claiming Elizabeth was nothing but a governess and was not worthy of being Mrs. Darcy."

Bingley frowned. "Caroline said such things about a gentleman's daughter?"

Darcy simply nodded his affirmation, as his friend blushed thoroughly.

Fitzwilliam said in heated tones, "And so, it is my fault?"

Darcy shook his head, again pitying his cousin's lack of insight. "I only pointed out what I did so you know, although this relationship is short-lived, I have never been more certain of anything or anyone in my life."

The colonel said in dutiful tones, "When will we be required to wish you happy?"

Darcy wanted to remark on his cousin's tone. Instead, he smiled easily. "I purchased an ordinary license on the evening I

159

arrived in Lambton. Mr. Brownstone will pronounce the vows on New Year's Eve."

Bingley was immediately reaching across the table to shake Darcy's hand again. "I shan't save my wishes for your happiness for the ceremony. Congratulations, ole chum!"

"Are you certain, Darcy?" his cousin asked. "I honestly believe an arrangement can be made—"

Darcy leaned across the table to catch his cousin's lapels in a tight tug. "I would suggest you swallow the remainder of your words. I am in love with Miss Bennet and she with me. My father fell in love with my mother over the course of a dance set, and they were happily married for fourteen years, and they would be so today if Lady Anne had not passed. Your own parents held an acquaintance of barely a month before Matlock came to an understanding with the countess. Moreover, we both know your mother's family were impoverished when Matlock married her, so do not dare to speak to me of Elizabeth's reduced circumstances. I do not require a settlement to make this marriage viable. I simply require Miss Bennet to share my vision for Pemberley, to be the mother of my children, and to be a safe harbor when I am adrift."

Elizabeth touched his shoulder, warning him he was in full view for all in the inn to watch. "The tea is hot. Let us enjoy it while we may. Should I pour?"

Darcy stood to hold the chair for her. "If you would be so kind, my dear."

Once she was seated, she calmly poured tea for each of them, preparing each cup to perfection, proving for all to see that she had been raised as a lady—a gentleman's daughter. It should have surprised Darcy how perfectly composed she appeared, but it did not, for he already knew her to be amazing. When she finished, she said evenly and in honest tones, "Colonel, I understand your concerns are for Mr. Darcy's future, but I promise you that your cousin possesses my deepest devotion."

"And you, mine," Darcy said as he caught her hand to place a kiss on her fingertips while eyeing his cousin with another warning glare.

After a short pause, the colonel raised his hands in surrender. "The two of you should expect the question of speed of your joining from more than one person," Fitzwilliam warned.

Elizabeth issued her own edict. "But not from those who supposedly love Mr. Darcy, as much as I do."

Fitzwilliam nodded his acceptance, but shrugged his response. "I do not expect Lady Catherine will be as willing to accept that you have chosen another wife. Matlock says the last time he called upon her at Rosings Park, our aunt had turned Anne's former quarters into some sort of shrine to the late Mrs. Darcy."

Elizabeth stiffened beside him. She placed her tea cup down with a decided thunk. "Rosings Park? As in the home of Lady Catherine de Bourgh?" She turned to him with horror marking her features. "Your late wife was Miss de Bourgh?"

"You know something of Anne?" he asked.

Elizabeth momentarily buried her face in her hands, before she straightened her shoulders to address him directly. "I took the acquaintance of your aunt and Miss de Bourgh the spring before my father's passing. The cousin who offered me his hand in marriage was, at that time, employed as Lady Catherine's clergyman."

Darcy and Fitzwilliam said together, "Mr. Collins?"

Darcy continued to exclaim, "Mr. Collins inherited your father's estate? That twit?"

Elizabeth dropped her eyes, a habit Darcy understood was necessary in her former occupation, but one he must quash before she appeared in public as his wife. "Twit or not, Mr. Collins is Longbourn's master, and my former friend, Charlotte Lucas, is now Mrs. Collins and is sleeping in the bed that once belonged to my mother."

Chapter sixteen

Darcy barked a laugh. "The twit who her ladyship insisted upon performing my marriage."

She looked up at him, all the humor gone from her features. "If you wish to—" she began with trembling lips.

"Do not dare to finish that sentence, Elizabeth Bennet. I shan't tolerate your doing so. We will marry on the eve of the New Year. Eventually, I will send Lady Catherine a letter to apprise her of the change in my marital disposition. It is likely her ladyship will initially lodge her objections, but I am certain Lord and Lady Matlock will speak to your goodness."

Fitzwilliam suggested, "Tell our aunt that Cassandra required a mother."

Bingley grinned widely. "Even better, why not tell Lady Catherine that you chose to keep Miss Anne's memory close by marrying the cousin of the man who performed your first marriage?"

Fitzwilliam also grinned. "You jest, Bingley, but Darcy's doing so could soften Lady Catherine's opinion more than you suspect."

Darcy declared, "*My* happiness does not depend on Lady Catherine's approval. It depends upon Miss Bennet's. Will you insist upon releasing me from my pledge?"

"Our marriage is truly your desire, sir?"

"You know it is."

"I wish it also," she said softly.

His cousin interrupted their exchange. "The countess was adamant that you return to Pemberley, Darcy. You do have a house full of guests and an annual ball to attend."

"Not without Miss Bennet," Darcy stated firmly. "What say you, Elizabeth?"

"Mr. Crownley's business will suffer if we depart," she said with a teasing smile.

"I will guarantee him bragging rights to how our marriage came about," he assured with a grin.

"Then, permit me to set Hannah to packing my portmanteau."

* * *

Darcy knew great satisfaction as he looked to his right to view Elizabeth at his side during supper. They had arrived at Pemberley when the ladies were all in their quarters preparing for supper and the gentlemen were in the billiards room or their quarters, also dressing.

He had sent Mrs. Reynolds to inform both the countess and Georgiana of his safe return to the house and that he would see them at supper.

He had been waiting by the door of the drawing room when Elizabeth had joined them. She appeared nervous, but she smiled up at him when she entered, as if she were thankful for his presence at her side.

"Miss Bennet, you have returned," the countess declared with a smile and a lift of her brows asking the question he intended to answer immediately.

"I departed Pemberley in search of Miss Bennet," he announced as the party looked on with a variety of expressions on their faces. "Fortunately, she had gone no farther than Lambton, for the public coach had been delayed by the storm." He caught Elizabeth's gloved hand and brought the back of it to his lips for a gentle kiss. He heard Miss Bingley gasp, but he did not turn his head to view the woman's distress, for, in truth, he did not require the lady's good opinion. More to the truth, Miss Bingley required his to remain in society, and Darcy had had enough of her vitriol to last a lifetime. "You each should be made aware that I have offered my hand in marriage to Miss Bennet. We will wed on the morning of the thirty-first, before the annual Pemberley ball that evening. I pray each of you will join in our happiness."

They were swarmed then with a plethora of well-wishes from all but Miss Bingley and her sister.

The countess tugged Elizabeth into a warm embrace, one Darcy assumed was genuine, but one also designed to demonstrate her ladyship's approval of their joining. He had no doubt that upon his party's return to Pemberley that Fitzwilliam had reported to his mother something of their discussion in Lambton; yet, in truth, Darcy had no care whether the Fitzwilliam faction of the family tree agreed with his marriage or not. It was time to call forth a bit of both Lady Anne Darcy and his father. They had defied the wishes of both their families to marry in perfect felicity. He would do the same if his relations did not stand with him.

* * *

Elizabeth did not believe her quarters at Pemberley would hold another soul. Mrs. Reynolds had brought Elizabeth a half-dozen dresses once belonging to the former Mrs. Darcy. Apologies were made, but Elizabeth cared not whether Mr. Darcy's late wife had worn the dresses once or a dozen times. She had enjoyed her brief time with Miss Anne de Bourgh at Rosings Park all those many years earlier, and, moreover, she approved of Mrs. Anne Darcy's taste in fabrics and the cut of the dresses. Since learning of the identity of the woman Mr. Darcy had married, Elizabeth had convinced herself that the late Mrs. Darcy would want William to be happy, for Miss de Bourgh had been such a gentle soul and very welcoming, and Elizabeth had set herself the task of seeing him happy for the remainder of their days together. Even if she did not love him, which she did most dearly, Fitzwilliam Darcy had earned her deepest respect, and she knew he deserved happiness more than all of her acquaintances. He was truly a good man.

"Mr. Darcy has ordered a dressmaker to call upon you after Christmastide," the housekeeper had explained.

"I am truly not offended," Elizabeth assured. "As I am one of five sisters, dresses made over were a common experience in my father's household. I truly believe the gesture proves Mr. Darcy's kindness is unlimited. Moreover, I understand that Mr. Darcy holds an exalted position in the neighborhood, and my appearance is a reflection on him."

Mrs. Reynolds nodded her head in apparent approval of Elizabeth's response. "What will you wear for the wedding?" she asked.

"I was considering the yellow silk," Elizabeth responded with a wistful sigh as she looked upon the gown Hannah had laid out on the bed. "And the red for the ball, if you do not believe it too 'scandalous.' The neckline is cut a bit lower than I am accustomed."

"I believe Mr. Darcy will not wish to be from your side when he views you in both the gowns. Your figure fits the style better than it did the late Mrs. Darcy, rest her soul."

Tears rushed to Elizabeth's eyes. "I keep thinking I shall wake up and find this is all a dream."

Mrs. Reynolds laughed easily. "It is a dream few will know, but you appear quite worthy of the distinction."

* * *

Thursday, 31 December 1818

The wedding ceremony proved to be all Elizabeth could have ever wanted. Mr. Darcy quashed the countess's desire for a larger ceremony and a grander presentation and the private chapel on the estate. The village turned out in droves to stand witness of their joining, as if they had all been part of the family, and, in many ways, they were, for Elizabeth realized Pemberley was not simply a great house, but it was the lifeblood of the village and the neighborhood. The responsibility she was assuming was more than a bit overwhelming, and, at times, she wished to flee, but, when she considered doing so, she would look to Mr. Darcy, and his smile would light up her world, telling her they were meant to be together. The day proved to be crisp and cold, but sunny, and everyone had cheered when she entered the church, for many within the crowd had had a hand in bringing her and Mr. Darcy together.

The changes to the yellow silk gown had turned out better than Elizabeth could hope, for, privately, she did not wish Mr. Darcy to be thinking of his late wife while he married her. Lace had been added to the bodice, as well as jewel-like beading on the sleeves, and, in her opinion, it was a breath-taking blend of romance and elegance. Not that Elizabeth could quite catch her breath: She was both nervous and calmly serene at the same time. It was as if all the mistakes she had made in her past were wiped away, and she was not thinking of the change in her status in society, but, rather, in the change in the way she saw the proverbial road she had been traveling: All the times she had taken a misstep had brought her to this moment and to her dearest William.

Hannah, along with Miss Darcy's maid, had managed to gather Elizabeth's straight wisps and had curled them into the most intricate design Elizabeth could have imagined, into which they had woven small yellow rose buds, gathered from the estate's conservatory, just for the occasion.

She had traveled to Lambton with the countess and Mr. Bingley, who had agreed to escort Elizabeth down the aisle. She wished she had had the opportunity to speak privately with Mr. Darcy this morning, but the household had been adamant that they remain apart until the time they were to speak their vows.

Although it would have been foolish to do so, she had desired to present him another opportunity to change his mind. Elizabeth was no fool: She knew she brought nothing of value to their marriage beyond her private promise to support her husband in all ways possible. It was he who was taking the risk, not she, and she wanted to provide him a chance to step away from his promise to her. Mr. Darcy was claiming a woman of whom he knew very little beyond the obvious attraction they held for each other.

However, before she could act upon her foolishness, the countess had called for her to escort her to the church, and she was now waiting in Mr. Brownstone's office for the ceremony. "Darcy is in place and waiting for his bride," Mr. Bingley announced when she opened the door at his knock on the office door.

"Is William as nervous as I?" she asked with a bit of worry.

Mr. Bingley chuckled. "Darcy is staring at the nave of the church where we will enter, and he has, generally, ignored everyone who has foolishly attempted to engage him in conversation."

"Meaning you, sir?" she said with a smile. Elizabeth had come to agree with Mr. Darcy: Mr. Bingley was too amiable for his own good.

"Darcy claims I am as chatty as a magpie," he admitted.

"Then we should remove the man from his misery." She placed her hand upon the gentleman's proffered arm. "Thank you, sir, for allaying my fears."

He bowed his head in acceptance of her compliment. "My pleasure, Miss Bennet."

"I believe, as you are serving in my father's stead on this most important day of my life, you should have the right to address me as 'Elizabeth.'"

"I would be honored." He looked at her in all seriousness. "If I may say so, you are strikingly beautiful today, as is proper for a bride."

"Do you believe Mr. Darcy will approve?" She asked one of the questions tormenting her.

"How could he not?" Mr. Bingley responded in what sounded to her of honest tones. He laid his gloved hand over hers, where it rested on his sleeve. "Being nervous is understandable, but I hold no doubt you and Darcy will do well together. You love each other—that is the first step. I like to think my own parents held such feelings for each other, and I hope to some day say the same of the woman I marry. It is my sincerest wish to one day view the expression of contentment I observe on Darcy's features when he looks at you plastered upon my own countenance when I look in the mirror."

"Mr. Darcy and I have had an acquaintance of less than a fortnight," she argued.

Mr. Bingley warned, "Do not question yourself, Miss Bennet. You are Darcy's choice. He has placed his heart and his trust in your hands. Protect both with the tenacity you used to survive your self-banishment from your family, and you two will do very well together."

"Mr. Darcy told you of my family's situation?" she asked with a raised eyebrow.

He grinned again. "I will share with you one important lesson I learned from Darcy when we were at university together: Servants in every well-managed house know all our secrets, my dear." He set their steps in motion. "Darcy awaits, and I know from experience, my friend is not a patient man. Just remember, all Darcy does for you he does, not out of obligation, but because he has truly fallen in love with you."

* * *

"Mr. Darcy," another of his guests said with a curtsey. Having Elizabeth beside him was proving more distracting than he had expected. They had returned to Pemberley for a smaller wedding breakfast than he had expected, especially with the countess in charge of the arrangements, but he suspected Lady Matlock and Mrs. Reynolds had had a long "discussion" in what would be appropriate under the circumstances. Apparently, Mrs. Reynolds had prevailed, and he was most thankful of the woman's understanding of his nature. Another dozen guests for the ball had arrived over the last couple of days, meaning some two dozen were in attendance when he and Elizabeth had arrived for the traditional celebration. However, if Darcy had had his choice, he would have marched his wife directly to their quarters and enjoyed the temptation she presented his sensibilities. That being said, he understood how people would judge them if he succumbed to his wishes.

Instead, after speaking their vows, they had made a brief appearance at the Rose and Crown to accept the personal well-wishes of many gathered there. Then, they had taken his carriage to Pemberley, assuaging some of his desires with a myriad of kisses—some light and playful, while others were more soul-claiming in nature.

After again accepting everyone's felicitations at the breakfast, Darcy had escorted her to her new quarters, where they had enjoyed intimacies twice and had lain in each other's arms and simply talked and napped and kissed in the manner of all lovers, a concept Darcy had never thought possible, for Anne was not of the nature of Elizabeth, and his future had not buried its roots in his heart until Elizabeth Bennet had quite literally walked across Pemberley's threshold. Most assuredly, in the nearly two years of his marriage to Anne, he had never once spent time in her bed beyond the need to perform his duty to her and their marriage. The novelty pleased him, for Elizabeth appeared to welcome his touch, which made him want to abandon their posts in the receiving line and return to her suite to take up where they had left off.

Even so, he said, "Good evening, Lady Bishop. I am pleased you and your family could join us this evening. Will Sir Henry be along shortly?"

"My husband is seeing to what appears to be a broken spoke on one of the carriage wheels. Your staff is assisting him. He should follow in a matter of minutes."

Darcy repeated the necessary words. "Good to know. For now, Lady Bishop, Miss Bishop, please accept the acquaintance of my wife, Mrs. Darcy."

The necessary greetings were pronounced as the Bishops extended their congratulations and continued through the receiving line. As he had done with each of those in line, Darcy had leaned to the side to provide Elizabeth more information on each of her new neighbors. "Sir Henry is Lady Bishop's second husband. Previously, she had married what others thought was below her station, despite her late husband's respectability: She married the local surgeon, but she lost both her husband and her son in flood waters when Mr. Ericks attempted to cross the swollen river to reach a patient requiring his services. She and her daughter moved away, I think to London, but Lady Bishop returned some ten years removed. The daughter had married a man in trade in London, and Mrs. Ericks had accepted Sir Henry's proposal and the care of his younger children."

"Mr. Ericks?" his wife questioned. "Do you recall Miss Ericks's Christian name?"

He looked at her in question. "I do not believe I ever heard her called anything other than 'Miss Ericks.'"

"Madeline?" she asked. "Was it Madeline?"

Darcy shrugged. "Possibly."

Without a notice of her intentions, Elizabeth stepped from the receiving line and followed Lady Bishop. Abandoning his post, Darcy followed, only to view Elizabeth catching Lady Bishop's arm. "Pardon," his wife said with some urgency. "I realize my actions may appear impertinent, and I likely," she glanced to him and smiled nervously, "have incurred the wrath of my new husband, but—" She looked again upon Lady Bishop. "I was wondering if you are an acquaintance of Mrs. Madeline Gardiner."

Lady Bishop looked oddly upon Elizabeth, but responded, nonetheless. "Madeline Gardiner is my eldest daughter. Why?"

Elizabeth reached to embrace the woman, but thought better of it. Instead, his wife presented Lady Bishop a proper curtsey. "Madeline Gardiner is my aunt. Her husband is my maternal uncle. You and I are, therefore, related by marriage."

Lady Bishop appeared as stunned as was he. Therefore, Darcy reached for Elizabeth's hand. "You must pardon my wife, Lady Bishop, for we must return to the receiving line. However, we will permit you time to consider Mrs. Darcy's announcement, and we will seek you out before the dancing begins."

"Certainly, Mr. Darcy," the woman said. "I am excited to hear more of what Mrs. Darcy means to share with me."

Darcy led Elizabeth back to their place in the receiving line, but, when he glanced to her, Elizabeth's chin was down, and she would not make eye contact with him. "Elizabeth," he whispered softly.

"I am grieved, sir," she said dutifully.

Darcy glanced about them to view those approaching and turned purposely to gather her close. "You have nothing," he said close to her ear, "for which to know sorrow. You have spent five years without a connection to another person in your life. I understand why you chased after Lady Bishop; yet, for now, your place is by my side. I am not reprimanding you. Rather, I am depending upon your natural vivaciousness to assist me in what is, generally, a painful exercise for a man of my nature."

She looked up at him in surprise. "I did not embarrass you/"

"A bit," he said with a smile, "but your actions can just as easily be attributed to your nervousness or your wonderment. On the other hand, I am often from step in social situations, and I require someone to ease my way."

She smiled fully then. "You do realize you should not embrace your wife in public."

He placed a quick kiss on her forehead. "I do, but, like the woman who holds my heart, I am sometimes impulsive. However, I am counting on you to provide me a reminder if I relapse."

"Gladly. As many times as is necessary." She stepped from his arms. "You may depend upon me, William. I have no notion of loving people in halves, it is not my nature."

"I instinctively recognized that fact the moment you first placed your hand upon my arm to enter Pemberley. My heart knew then that you were mine."

* * *

It was nearly two of the clock when Darcy had said his farewells and followed Elizabeth to their quarters. As promised, they had spoken privately to Lady Bishop, who begged Elizabeth for any news of Mrs. Gardiner. Because of their duties, they could not spend the evening with the woman, but Elizabeth made arrangements to call upon her after Twelfth Night. Meanwhile, Darcy suggested that he invite the Gardiners and others of Elizabeth's family to Pemberley in the spring. All readily agreed, and his wife was bubbling happy for the remainder of the evening, pleasing him equally as well as his offer had done for her.

"Where are you, love?" he called when he found her quarters empty.

"Here." Her voice came from the direction of the balcony.

He crossed the room to the open door. "What are you doing outside? Are you not cold?"

She smiled that special smile, meant purely for him. "I thought you might keep me warm, husband," she said with a teasing lift of her brows. "Are you up to the task?"

She looked enticingly over her shoulder at him. The lacing of her gown had been loosened, and the material had slipped slightly from her shoulders. Moreover, her hair had broken free of the simple chignon she had worn to the ball, with strands brushing against her neck. In his opinion, she was magnificent.

"I will attempt to provide the necessary warmth, Mrs. Darcy," he said as he wrapped his arms about her waist to tug her backside against his front, while he placed a line of kisses along the curve of her neck and her collarbone. "You did not tell me why we are in the cold when we should be in a nice warm bed," he whispered against her skin.

172

She giggled sweetly. "I fear, sir, you have married a vain woman. As I have never owned any jewelry other than a pearl necklace and a brooch that once belonged to my Grandmother Bennet, I have taken it upon myself to judge the many rings you presented me in the moonlight to determine if the jewels glow as lovely under the moonlight as they do in, say, a ballroom."

"And do they?" His mind cared not for jewels. It had only one thought: her body and his joining again.

She sighed wistfully. "They did not; yet, the moonlight has others powers. Look how beautiful Pemberley appears with the snow on the trees and ground. It is so lovely; I wish I could capture it as such in paints. You own a place of such spectacular magic, William. I fully understand your fierce loyalty to it. Thank you for permitting me to be a part of Pemberley's future. I am truly honored by your trust in me."

His wife, as yet, did not understand what a great compliment she had presented him, but, some day, she would. She had already identified the core of him. The essence of Pemberley flowed through his veins. It was his lifeblood, as was she. Although people would doubt the strength of the love he felt for her, for their acquaintance had been of short duration, it was as real as his devotion to this land.

He bent to lift her to him. "Let us see what the candlelight does for the emerald in your ring."

She laid her head against his chest. "I adore my new life, William," she said softly.

"And I adore you, Elizabeth Bennet Darcy. Together we will disprove the naysayers who do not understand that happiness does not come from expectations of its arrival, but rather from the acceptance of the delight in its timely appearance. I do not wish to wait for it—to postpone it until the future. Life is too short to wake each day with regrets. So, I choose to love deeply and to live with you by my side and in my heart."

epilogue

Saturday, 30 December 1848

Darcy looked across the dance floor to where his wife of thirty years hugged their youngest child. Elizabeth had presented him four more children: three sons and another daughter. Five children, including Cassandra, in total. His oldest had called Elizabeth "mama" from the time since she was about two years of age, and his wife had shown no favoritism in the rearing of his daughter with Anne. Elizabeth had opened up her heart to his child, as she had opened up her heart to him. Their Cassandra had married Lord Jasper's son some ten years back; someday, his and Anne's sweet, soft-spoken child would be a viscountess. They had been blessed with three children, and Darcy often commented how Lady Catherine and Anne must be doing some sort of happy jig in Heaven as they looked down upon Cassandra.

His eldest son, Bennet, would inherit Pemberley, and the future of the estate had been secured by his and Elizabeth's second grandchild, a boy named "Fitzwilliam Darcy." Despite all the accolades he had known in his lifetime, viewing his blood running through the veins of his children and grandchildren was, in Darcy's estimation, the greatest honors he would ever claim. Bennet and his Abigail were expecting their third child in April. Young Fitzwilliam and Matthew Darcy were the current residents of Pemberley's nursery and school rooms.

Bennet had been followed in quick succession by Oliver, George, and Jane. He and his "dearest, loveliest Elizabeth" had produced a child with some degree of regularity, somewhere between sixteen and twenty months apart, in those first few years of marriage.

However, when he had come close to losing Elizabeth with the fifth child—their child born dead and her being required to carry it to term, Darcy had privately thanked God for permitting her to live, while making a promise he would ask for no more from the Lord's benevolence. He thought Elizabeth might bleed to death, but, fortunately, a skilled surgeon from Scotland had saved her life; yet, the man had told them she would never carry another child, for she was too scarred inside for them to conceive another. For a long while, Darcy feared his lovely Elizabeth might grieve herself to death, but, eventually, she walked in the sunlight again and became the other half of his soul. Thankfully, she was not made for melancholy.

Their daughter Jane had announced her engagement to Sir Lawrence Chandler this evening. By summer, his youngest would be a baronetess. He had fallen instantly in love with his elfin daughter when he first laid eyes on the child, for Jane Elizabeth Georgiana Darcy was a perfect image of her mother. Soon she would place her hand in another's and leave Pemberley for a different man's house. The idea saddened Darcy more than he would care to admit, even to himself.

Over the years, many from that first Christmastide he and Elizabeth spent together had also joined forces. His cousin had married Georgiana, and Darcy was uncle to their two children: a daughter and a son. His dear sister had suffered greatly with her choice, for he and the countess had rightly predicted the fact that the colonel had seen too much of war to make life easy for any of them. However, the colonel and Georgiana had come to an agreement of sorts, one that brought them both apparent satisfaction. From what Darcy could tell, they were as happy together as most marriages of their society.

Bingley had fallen heels over head in love with Elizabeth's sister Jane Bennet. They lived some thirty miles removed from Pemberley and had two sons and a daughter. Unfortunately for Miss Bingley, she had not married until she was nearing thirty years of age, and, then, it was to a wealthy businessman who was one of Bingley's partners.

Miss Davidson finally earned Mr. Whalen's attention. They married a year after Darcy and Elizabeth. Captain Stewart originally proposed to Miss Whalen, but, when refused, Mary Bennet caught the captain's notice. They settled in York on the estate Stewart had inherited from an uncle. Their children numbered five.

Ironically, over the years, all those who had stood witness to his and Elizabeth's successful marriage, had either proposed to their mates at the annual Pemberley ball or came to an understanding with the significant person in their lives on that evening. Three of his and Elizabeth's children had announced their proposals on the evening of the annual ball.

Much to Elizabeth's sadness, Mrs. Bennet had passed some ten years earlier. She had died in the cottage Darcy and Bingley had purchased for her. Elizabeth's youngest sisters had made marriages among the men of the neighborhood about Meryton. Lydia's comely features and spontaneity had caught the eye of the eldest son of Mrs. Bennet's long-time friend, Mrs. Long. They had settled in the Long's estate house, when Mr. Harold Long passed. They were both quite "silly" in Elizabeth's opinion, but she admitted they made a handsome pair and their personalities were quite compatible. When they were both alive, Mrs. Bennet and Mrs. Long spent many happy days together singing the praises of the match.

Miss Kitty had married John Lucas, the son of their most prominent neighbor. Mrs. Bennet thought it justice to place her daughter as the mistress of Lucas Lodge, as the former Charlotte Lucas had become the mistress of Longbourn. Although Elizabeth often commented on how it was God's way of righting what had happened to her family, Charlotte Collins, like her predecessor at Longbourn, had delivered only daughters for her husband, Mr. Collins, effectively ending the entailment. Darcy had purchased the estate for Oliver, which pleased Elizabeth greatly to have her son in the home in which she and his aunts had been born.

Darcy had found another small estate for George. It was some twenty miles removed from Georgiana, and Darcy's youngest son spent a great deal of his time with his aunt and the colonel. Georgiana was playing matchmaker to George, but his youngest son had yet to speak his proposal to any of Georgiana's suggested mates for her nephew.

"A pence for your thoughts, Father," Bennet said from his place beside Darcy.

Darcy turned to look fondly on his eldest. "I was simply considering how fully God has blessed me and mine, as well as the fact all my good fortune rests in my marriage to your mother."

His eldest son chuckled, "We all had a bet on this evening. We knew you would be feeling sentimental. After all, at midnight, you and mother have been together for thirty years."

Darcy smiled easily. "It feels like only yesterday that I was waiting impatiently for Elizabeth's appearance at the Lambton church."

Bennet placed his hand on Darcy's shoulder. "Come along, your children have a surprise for you and mother."

His son strode to the raised dais to face the crowd gathered in Pemberley's ballroom. "May I have your attention, please?" he said in a loud voice to quieten the crowd.

Their guests moved closer, and Darcy found himself standing at the front of the crowd. He was about to turn to search for his wife, but Elizabeth slipped in beside him and claimed his hand. As always, she was his anchor.

Bennet continued, "Might my brothers and sisters join me on the dais?"

From behind him, each of his children squeezed past him to join their brother.

Bennet continued to speak for the group. "It is nearing midnight, and, tomorrow, we will welcome in another new year together. Normally, we would celebrate on the Eve of the New Year, but the Church of England might frown on such festivities on a Sunday." Those among the crowd chuckled and lifted their glasses in a toast to Bennet's truth. "Most gathered here tonight have come to this place at this time of year to celebrate the renewal of life. Yet, before we do just that, we five," and he gestured to his brothers and sisters, "wish to speak of your host and hostess. At midnight tonight, they will be celebrating thirty years of marriage, for tomorrow will be the anniversary of their first Pemberley ball together." Applause rose from the crowd around him, and more than one person patted Darcy on the back in a congratulatory manner.

Cassandra spoke next, "Each of us has learned hard lessons at the hands of our father and mother, and I am not speaking of the switch Papa employed twice with Oliver." She smiled at her brother, who blushed. "Believe me, our parents considered not having other children after Oliver came along."

"That is not true," Darcy declared loudly.

His wife laughed easily. "Oliver and Mr. Darcy's character are one and the same," she shared. "The apple and the tree and all those other sayings about fathers and sons prove true. Sometimes the two did not see things from the same perspective. Yet, Mr. Darcy knew as much pain with the punishment as did our son. Moreover, pouring ink on Cassandra's hair required more than a simple admonishment."

Cassandra kept the floor. "I do suppose I teased Ollie more than I should have." She sobered quickly to look upon him and Elizabeth. "From my parents, I learned that love takes work. It requires joining together to overcome every obstacle placed in one's way. It is facing life's complications, standing hand-in-hand, as Fitzwilliam and Elizabeth Darcy have done every day of their life, and as they do now."

Bennet cleared his throat before speaking his part. "We do not wish anyone to think our parents have traveled an easy road. They have known hardships and loss, as have we all. No one tending such an estate as is Pemberley, especially through the years following the wars we have known for the last thirty years, can ponder long without thinking of some hardships, but my parents have risen above much of it—but not without great sacrifice on their parts. They practiced what they believed was the core of their relationship. They remained cognizant of the need to know happiness by claiming every moment with love and grace and gratitude and not taking any day together for granted or viewing their next day together as a guarantee."

Oliver stepped forward. "As you have heard the others say, I am very much like Fitzwilliam Darcy in the way I view the world. Therefore, I can tell you, without a doubt, my father, and my mother, have taught me, not only with words, for I am not the type to believe all that I hear, but through the way they have lived their lives, that I must abandon any ideas of what I thought the world owed me as a

179

Darcy. Rather, I have learned to celebrate my blessings and never forget there are those who require a hand up to reach their own potential. Happiness can be fleeting. It comes and goes with some regularity, but the promise of a better future is there for those willing to work hard and never place themselves above others."

George grinned widely as it was his turn. "Oliver and I should have discussed what to say, for he stole the words right out of my mouth." The gathered crowd around them chuckled. "I planned to say something of how our parents taught each of us to accept how life presents itself and to make the most of the opportunities when they arrive. A person's worth has nothing to do with the size of his purse. It is what one chooses to do with his life that matters—a person must learn to be happy with his choices. That is the first lesson each of us learned from Fitzwilliam and Elizabeth Darcy. If a person is happy with his choices, everything else will fall in place."

Jane spoke last. "From my mother, I learned life was too short to cry over what cannot be changed. I can honestly say, it is rare to view my mother without a smile, especially for each of her children and always—always, for our father."

George added, "However, if you do encounter Elizabeth Darcy and she is not smiling, run for the hills."

Darcy squeezed his wife's hand in companionship. Their son's words were true. It was rare that he or his children had been on the receiving end of her ire, but when it was so, they walked lightly around her until *his* Elizabeth found her way to them again.

Jane continued, "My parents have known happiness together, not because life was always easy, but because they knew harmony in their thoughts and opinions, in their speech, and in their deeds."

By the time Jane was finished, Darcy's eyes were filled with tears, but a smile lifted his lips. He and Elizabeth had raised five remarkable children. Even so, he knew his wife would require a handkerchief before he did. He reached in his inside pocket and handed her one.

She laughingly swatted at his chest. "You know me too well, sir," she murmured through happy tears. "I am a watering pot, William."

He slid his arm about her waist and pulled her closer to him to kiss her forehead. "You are my watering pot, love."

Bennet claimed the crowd's attention again. "It is with immense pride and love that we wish our parents twice the happiness they have known these last thirty years and ask them to lead us in the final celebratory waltz of 1848. I doubt the rest of us will care, but I can guarantee they will have a private dance to mark the beginning of year thirty-one of a long and happy life together tomorrow evening while the rest of us snore away the hours waiting for 1849 to official." Again, everyone around them laughed and clapped in approval.

Bennet gestured to the musicians, and the first strands of the music could be heard above shuffling feet as the crowd parted to permit him and Elizabeth the center of the floor.

Darcy bowed to his lovely wife. "Might I claim this dance, Mrs. Darcy?' She placed her hand in his, and he led her to the middle of the floor, took her into his arms, and set their steps into a proper waltz. "Our children made us sound as if we were perfect."

"We are perfectly ordinary," Elizabeth corrected.

"Yet, perfectly suited for each other," Darcy countered.

As the other guests joined them on the dance floor to welcome in the new year a day early, Darcy spun Elizabeth to a halt. "Our many imperfections have brought me the most joyous moments of my life. I love you, Elizabeth Darcy."

"The secret of any happy marriage," she said as she snuggled deeper into his embrace, "is to marry the one you love. We began our journey with a glance and a touch and a smile and, finally, a kiss."

"And a village and the estate servants set on bringing us together," he said as he lowered his head to claim her mouth. The kiss continued longer than was proper for polite society, and neither Darcy nor Elizabeth heard the second round of applause. As was customary for them, they were lost to each other. They had loved each other from their first day together, but not in the same manner as they loved each other now. They were more than lovers. Two truly had become one. They were each other's heart mate.

~ Finis ~

Excerpt from *Obsession: A Superheroine's Novel*
Arriving March 2022

Chapter One

London, late April 1802

"Relax your shoulders and lift your chin," her uncle warned under his breath, as they entered the line of those awaiting admittance into Lord and Lady Godfrey's grand masquerade.

"Yes, sir," she responded by swallowing the nervousness spreading steadily through her chest. This was Audrey's first foray into English society, and she did not want to disappoint her uncle, for it had been he who had instructed her in how to create the most gossip possible, leaving a bold impression on all who viewed her. This was more than a bit confusing to her, for others avoided any marked recognition, but she would never question any of Uncle Jacobi's decisions. However, from what she knew of English society, even in a mask, she should be presented as a potential virginal bride, especially if her uncle desired the proper connections, which he did. In truth, she did not know why her Uncle Jacobi wished her to create a scene; however, she owed him much and would not wish to know his disfavor. More importantly, she could never repay him for the gift of his protection when Audrey had been her most vulnerable.

She wore red, the color of a fallen woman, when, in reality, she had never known a man, not in the carnal sense of the word, nor even as a friend. Naturally, Audrey was familiar with a number of men, for her uncle had an unacknowledged army serving him, and, therefore, serving her, as well. Yet, not "servants" in the exact sense of the word as it was used in England. Audrey was well aware, back in France, her Uncle Jacobi had many employed to do his biding, and she suspected also to watch her every move, especially since their arrival in England from the Continent. Audrey did not know exactly how to explain when things between her and her uncle had changed, but they had. At times, it also felt as if he considered her to be his enemy, which she most assuredly was not: She owed her uncle her life.

"Lord Honfleur," Lady Godfrey said with a twitter of obvious delight, for the woman would claim the pleasure of saying she was the first hostess to entertain the Marquis of Honfleur's presence at her fête.

"My lady." Her uncle bowed over the woman's hand, offering an air kiss several inches above her ladyship's gloved knuckles for effect. *"Merci de m'avoir reçu.* I be much honored by your reception."

The woman trilled her response. "I am equally honored, my lord."

Uncle Jacobi tugged Audrey closer to his side, but he continued to speak to Lady Godfrey. "Pardon, madam. *Mon anglais n'est pas aussi parfait que je le sou haiterais.* My English not so perfect."

Audrey wondered why her uncle would declare himself not able to speak English well, for he was English by birth, or so she was led to believe; yet, she swallowed the remark rushing to her lips.

Honfleur continued in what could only be called a pretense of broken English. "Madam, I mean, my lady, *permettez-moi*, to present *ma nièce*, Miss Moreau."

Lady Godfrey reached out a hand to Audrey. "Are you not the most handsome of ladies. Lord Honfleur will require a sharp sword to keep the young bucks from whisking you away."

Audrey could defend herself with a variety of weapons; yet, she said in a slow, exaggerated enunciation demanded of her by her uncle, "The . . . honor . . . is . . . mine . . . my lady."

The people behind them edged closer, and Lady Godfrey frowned at their forwardness, but she gestured toward the ballroom. "Please enjoy yourself."

Uncle Jacobi led Audrey in a bow of parting, and they walked away together. "You did well, my dear," he whispered. His encouragement was welcomed by her fearful heart. This was, quite literally, her first venture into society, and she did not know what to expect.

"Thank you, sir."

He quietly continued to instruct her as Lady Godfrey's butler announced them to those gathered in the ballroom. Tonight was to be an exercise in seeing and being seen in return. As expected, all eyes turned their way, and Audrey forced herself not to reach for her mask and to know assurance it had not slipped down.

Her uncle had had the mask created especially for his daughter, Caroline, but, as Caroline's voyage to England had been delayed, Uncle Jacobi had pressed Audrey into service. The mask was red and gold to match the gown Audrey wore—all meant for Caroline, for they would have made a remarkable statement upon her cousin's svelte body and would have complemented Caroline's coal black hair. He had instructed the maid Mathild on every detail of Audrey's appearance, just as, in the past, he had crafted every facet of Audrey's life.

"Despite your red hair taking away from the effect the costume will generate," he had said in his customary critical tones, "I wish you to be the semblance of an exotic flower."

Therefore, Mathild had used a pencil whose tip had been dipped in an oil to create a weblike design about Audrey's eyes, providing the illusion of Audrey wearing a mask even when the red and gold one she held in her hand had been removed. The markings had hurt as they were put in place, and Audrey wondered it she would ever be able to scrub them off without removing part of her skin. Mathild had even used a special paint from the Orient to decorate Audrey's nails—not that she planned to remove her gloves unless her uncle insisted upon her doing so. She supposed such would be required at supper, but she had the distinct impression she and her uncle would be leaving before then.

As her eyes scanned the throngs of people scattered about the room, they landed upon the countenance of a man, whose gaze studied her intently. She could not determine whether his assessment was one of approval or condemnation, but, for the first time in more years than she could recall, she wanted to know what someone, other than her uncle, thought of her.

The man's hair was russet—a dark brown with a reddish-orange tent. He had broad shoulders and was well-dressed. Trim waist. A physique indicating regular time spent in sport. The mask in his gloved hand matched his waistcoat and his gloves, all of which complemented his appearance of elegance, mixed with rugged abandon, for his cravat sat a bit askew, as if he had tugged on it several times. The idea pleased her: She would not have him be too perfect.

Yet, despite his pleasing countenance, Audrey felt nothing but curiosity. *At least, the emotion is the first genuine one I have experienced in more than a dozen years. It is not one dictated by my uncle or expected of her by Caroline,* she thought with a touch of disappointment, for all the books she had read had her thinking she would fall in love at first sight with such a man.

"The Earl of Marksman," her uncle whispered.

"Pardon?" Audrey asked, belatedly realizing her uncle had taken note of her interest in the gentleman.

"The man who has caught your attention, my dear," he said under his breath. "I would prefer you avoid him."

Audrey never quite understood how her uncle appeared to know everyone, but she did not dare ask. "I simply took note of how the strutting peacock chose a mask to match his waistcoat," she assured.

"Naturally," Uncle Jacobi murmured in what sounded of approval, a sentiment he rarely expressed when it came to her. Audrey had become accustomed to knowing his disappointment. Sometimes she wondered why he had gone to all the trouble to retrieve her from where her mother had left her. Not that she was unthankful for the life he had provided her, but she wished for someone to treat her as more than an obligation. He tilted his head so he might speak more privately. "Do not become too distracted by the pomp and pageantry displayed here this evening," he warned. "You have a role to play in this evening's foray. You must not forget your purpose at my side."

"I understand, Uncle," she was quick to say. "I await your instructions."

* * *

"Place your eyes back in your head," Theodora said from somewhere off Alexander's right shoulder. For the life of him, Alexander could not withdraw his eyes from the woman who had been introduced to the room as "Miss Moreau."

186

"It is not as you assume, Theodora," he murmured. "There is something about her which draws the eye."

Dora tutted her disapproval. "Perhaps such be because the woman be dressed as a lady found in a sheik's tent rather than an English country shepherdess."

Alexander smiled easily as he turned to his long-time companion. "She is a bold one."

"And you be enjoying 'bold,' too much," Theodora said in cold bitterness.

It was then Alexander took note of Dora's evident jealousy. Although he and Theodora had never actually spoken of a future together, an odd "understanding," of sorts, existed between them. They were very much inseparable—had been so since they were each coming into their teen years. From the time when Alexander had inherited the Marksman earldom—since the time Theodora's father, Lord Duncan, had become one of Alexander's guardians. Lord Duncan had paved the way for Alexander's rise from abject poverty to one of the most influential earldoms in the realm.

He turned to look upon Dora's familiar face. "I do enjoy bold," he said with a smile. "Such is why you and I have an inseparable bond."

Dora frowned. "Don't ye attempt to bam me, Marksman," she warned in a tone he had heard often over the years.

"Not in my nature," he assured. Yet, when his eyes returned to the stranger, Dora huffed her displeasure and stormed away.

"See ye've irritated me daughter again, Marksman," Lord Duncan said with a chuckle. "Ye've a way of constantly keepin' Theodora off step."

Alexander ignored the implications, for he was not yet ready to speak a proposal to Dora or to any woman. His work for the Crown took precedence. Times were too turbulent to speak words of "forever" to another. "For now, tell me what you know of the Marquis of Honfleur."

"Not much," Duncan said in confidence. "We've men verifying his legitimacy, but haven't heard back from those in France. His 'supposed' marquisate would be quite removed."

Alexander smiled upon his mentor. Lord Duncan had lived the majority of his life in England, but bits of the man's Scottish roots colored his lordship's speech and, therefore, Theodora's also. "So we are blind in this matter?"

"Been blind more than once," Duncan remarked.

"And the young woman at his side?" Alexander asked. For some yet to be explained reason, he prayed the lady was not Honfleur's wife.

"Honfleur's niece," Duncan explained. "Be surprised his daughter not be upon his arm. From what we know, the man rarely travels anywhere without his daughter."

"Daughter?" Alexander asked. "No wife?"

"The daughter's name be 'Caroline,'" Duncan explained. "No one be knowing anything of the marquis's wife. The daughter be customarily at her father's side. Other than from a distance, no one has much seen the niece."

"More well trained than the daughter or less? From what you shared previously, the daughter's 'studies' have been unconventional," Alexander suggested. "Has the marquis included the niece in these 'accomplishments'?"

"I be imagining we be soon discovering for ourselves, for the young lady has stepped away from the marquis's side."

Alexander glanced to where the woman made her way through the crush of guests gathered in Lady Godfrey's ballroom. Behind him, musicians tuned their instruments. "Let us see if I cannot detain the lady from whatever is her mission this evening. You keep an eye on Honfleur."

"Theodora?" Duncan asked in warning of his daughter's reaction.

"Inform Dora this is strictly business," Alexander said with a knowing grin.

"Haven't ye learnt, boy, it is not in yer best interest to ire a Scottish girl?" Duncan challenged.

Alexander's smile widened. "I have never been known to possess sensibilities."

"Aye, ye've not. I'll watch Honfleur. See what the French lass be about," Duncan assured.

188

Alexander nodded and moved away, circling in the opposite direction of the young woman, who moved stealthily through the throng. She periodically turned away to study a sculpture or painting so others would pass her by, meaning she had been instructed not to draw too much attention, although her costume was most provoking and certainly had earned his attention and he imagine that of half the men in attendance. Yet, not all were put off by her guise, for, out of the corner of his eye, he noted how Lord Bacggart was quickly making his way toward the woman. Even so, Alexander did not increase his speed, but he did adjust his course in order to reach the woman before the viscount.

Unfortunately, Theodora stepped before him, blocking his way. "I thought we were to share the first set," she accused.

"I do not recall requesting your hand for the set," Alexander said with more calm than he felt. Although he adored Dora, he knew she could create quite the scene if provoked too far, and, at the moment, he did not want others to know his business. He wished to have Honfleur's niece close enough so they might converse without her uncle's interference.

Theodora blushed and her chin dropped in embarrassment. "We always—"

Alexander squeezed the back of her hand to cut short her protest. "This is not personal, Dora. Now, do not engender the gossips with your actions. We will both regret what has transpired, if such is so."

He knew she wished to protest, for Scottish girls were, generally, not the type to bend easily to a man's will, but after an elongated pause, she said, "Fine," in that particular tone, which any man who dared to woo a hot-tempered lass, knew meant, "I hope to see you rot in Hell's fire, and, when such occurs, do not dare to beg me for a glass of water." With a curtsey that reeked of defiance, she walked away.

Alexander watched her for a few brief seconds. Dora was fiercely loyal to those she affected, and, if he dared to admit them, which he would not, he held tender feelings for the lass, but there were times he wished for something different for his future.

With a sigh of resignation, he turned his attention again to the mystery woman. Bacggart had reached her side and was bowing before her. Alexander doubted Bacggart would claim the woman's hand, even if she would be expected to sit out the remaining sets after her refusal: If she truly was Honfleur's niece, she had not made an appearance this evening in hopes of gaining a suitor.

As he neared the pair, he heard Bacggart say, "Would you honor me with this set, my lady?"

Before she could respond, Alexander stepped between them to say, "I apologize, my dear. I was momentarily detained, and it grieves me it was necessary for you to search me out in the room. I should have been more prompt in reaching your side. Are you prepared for our dance?"

Her eyes widened in obvious alarm. She glanced to where Honfleur held court and then to him and Bacggart. "I meant to seek some air, my lord," she said softly, in better English than he had expected from a "French" girl. Perhaps Bacggart did not recognize the fear lacing her words, but Alexander did, and he suddenly felt a sense of protectiveness toward her.

"We might walk the room instead, Miss Moreau, if it pleases you, or we might step out onto the balcony. Naturally, just outside the door where you may still be viewed by your uncle."

She swallowed hard before responding, "I believe my uncle would prefer I did not step out on the balcony."

Alexander presented the woman his best smile. "If you insist." He offered her his arm and nodded a farewell to Bacggart. He recognized the viscount's dismay, but in the "pecking order" that was London's society, Alexander's earldom held the advantage of both history and peerage.

Although her hand barely touched the cloth of his sleeve, Alexander noted a certain "comfort" in having her at his side. It was something he had never considered with anyone previously, and the idea would require more attention once he was alone. For now, he would be required to concentrate on learning all he could of the woman and her uncle.

They walked in silence for perhaps a quarter of the room before she said, "I do not recall your requesting a dance, my lord."

Again, his awareness was on alert, for a slight quiver in her voice announced her nervousness. She was most assuredly not the polished "agent" her uncle appeared to be. Perhaps Alexander could use such information to learn more of Honfleur's purpose in England.

"I would never permit a lady to suffer thirty minutes of Lord Bacggart stepping upon her toes. I meant to be your gallant."

"Do you not think I am capable of refusing Lord Bacggart without your interference, my lord?"

He grinned purposely. "Here I thought myself providing a service to a stranger in our fair land." He faked a blow to his heart.

"Do not be foolish, my lord," she chastised, although the slight blush coloring her cheeks said she was more embarrassed than angry.

"I assure you, Miss Moreau, I am never foolish. I am always honest. It was my intention to claim your acquaintance, but Lord Bacggart managed to reach you first. A grand gesture was required," he declared.

She had, at length, found her courage. "You made no effort to greet my uncle or me upon our entrance, and you were detained by the beautiful lady in the blue shepherdess's dress."

Alexander did not look away from the woman at his side. The fact she had noted his companions spoke volumes. Whoever she was, she had been trained in observation, and he suspected in other forms of engagements. "The lady is the daughter of my nearest neighbor. Her father's estate and mine march along together. We have known each other since we were quite young. In fact, Lord Duncan served as one of my guardians when I became Marksman. Until I reached my majority."

"Does Lord Duncan no longer provide sage advice?" she asked, uncharacteristically forgetting the "chess match" they played.

"Duncan remains as steadfast as ever," he confided. It was not like him to discuss his relationship with the Scot beyond the long-forgotten guardianship, but, for a reason he could not explain, Alexander wished her to know more of him and him of her.

The first notes of the music sounded, interrupting the moment. "Do we dance, Miss Moreau, or not?" he asked with a lift of eyebrows.

She glanced to where Honfleur kept company with several of those in Parliament who possessed more "radical" views. "My uncle will not approve," she said in tones which again relayed a certain underlying "fear."

Her reaction had Alexander suddenly feeling very protective of her. "I would not wish you to know censure on my account, Miss Moreau. I would gladly return you to your uncle's side, if such is your wish."

She shook off his offer. "I am not likely to know peace whether I choose to dance or not," she announced. "In truth, I have always dreamed of dancing in an English ballroom. When I was young, my mother would spin me around and around and hum some of her favorite songs as we danced about each other."

"I had a mother who did something very similar," he said with an easy smile, for that particular memory was one of his favorites of Madelyn Smithfield Dutton. He extended his hand to her. "One dance in honor of our mothers."

She placed her hand in his, and, instantly, another shock of awareness skittered up Alexander's arm. It was only through a force of will he did not jerk his hand away. Then he looked into the lady's eyes and read the same reaction in hers.

"What the devil?" he hissed.

Other Novels by Regina Jeffers

Jane Austen-Inspired Novels:
Darcy's Passions: Pride and Prejudice Retold Through His Eyes
Darcy's Temptation: A Pride and Prejudice Sequel
Captain Frederick Wentworth's Persuasion: Jane Austen's Classic Through His Eyes
Vampire Darcy's Desire: A Pride and Prejudice Paranormal Adventure
The Phantom of Pemberley: A Pride and Prejudice Mystery
Christmas at Pemberley: A Pride and Prejudice Holiday Sequel
The Disappearance of Georgiana Darcy: A Pride and Prejudice Mystery
The Mysterious Death of Mr. Darcy: A Pride and Prejudice Mystery
The Prosecution of Mr. Darcy's Cousin: A Pride and Prejudice Mystery
Mr. Darcy's Fault: A Pride and Prejudice Vagary
Mr. Darcy's Present: A Pride and Prejudice Holiday Vagary
Mr. Darcy's Bargain: A Pride and Prejudice Vagary
Mr. Darcy's Brides: A Pride and Prejudice Vagary
Mr. Darcy's Bet: A Pride and Prejudice Vagary
Elizabeth Bennet's Deception: A Pride and Prejudice Vagary
Elizabeth Bennet's Excellent Adventure: A Pride and Prejudice Vagary
The Pemberley Ball: A Pride and Prejudice Vagary
A Dance with Mr. Darcy: A Pride and Prejudice Vagary
The Road to Understanding: A Pride and Prejudice Vagary
Pride and Prejudice and a Shakespearean Scholar: A Pride and Prejudice Vagary
Where There's a FitzWILLiam Darcy, There's a Way: A Pride and Prejudice Vagary
In Want of a Wife: A Pride and Prejudice Vagary
Losing Lizzy: A Pride and Prejudice Vagary
The Mistress of Rosing Park: A Pride and Prejudice Vagary
Pemberley's Christmas Governess: A Pride and Prejudice Vagary
Honor and Hope: A Contemporary Pride and Prejudice

Regency and Contemporary Romances:
The Scandal of Lady Eleanor, Book 1 of the Realm Series (aka A Touch of Scandal)
A Touch of Velvet, Book 2 of the Realm Series
A Touch of Cashémere, Book 3 of the Realm Series
A Touch of Grace, Book 4 of the Realm Series

A Touch of Mercy, Book 5 of the Realm Series
A Touch of Love, Book 6 of the Realm Series
A Touch of Honor, Book 7 of the Realm Series
A Touch of Emerald, The Conclusion of the Realm Series
His American Heartsong: A Companion Novel to the Realm Series
His Irish Eve
Angel Comes to the Devil's Keep, Book 1 of the "Twins" Trilogy
The Earl Claims His Comfort, Book 2 of the "Twins" Trilogy
Lady Chandler's Sister, Book 3 of the "Twins" Trilogy
The Heartless Earl: A Common Elements Romance Project Novel
Lady Joy and the Earl: A Regency Christmas Romance
Letters from Home: A Regency Christmas Romance
Courting Lord Whitmire: A Regency May-December Romance
Last Woman Standing: A Regency Christmas Romance
The Courtship of Lord Blackhurst: A Regency Romance
Lord Radcliffe's Best Friend: A Regency Romance
The Jewel Thief and the Earl: A Regency Romance
His Christmas Violet: A Regency "Change of Life" Romance
I Shot the Sheriff: A Tragic Heroes in Classic Lit Series Novel
Captain Stanwick's Bride: A Tragic Heroes in Classic Lit Series Novel
Beautified by Love
Something in the Air
Escape to Romance
Christmas Ever After: A Clean Regency Romance Anthology
Regency Summer Escape Anthology
A Regency Christmas Proposal Anthology
Regency Summer Secrets and Soirées Anthology
A Regency Christmas Together Anthology
Regency Mid-Summer Mischief Anthology
A Regency Christmas Correspondence Anthology
Second Chances: The Courtship Wars
One Minute Past Christmas, A Holiday Short Story

Coming Soon…
Indentured Love: A Persuasion Vagary
Obsession (Early 2022)
Mr. Darcy's Inadvertent Wife (2022)

Meet Regina Jeffers

Writing passionately comes easily to Regina Jeffers. A master teacher, for thirty-nine years, she passionately taught thousands of students English in the public schools of West Virginia, Ohio, and North Carolina. Yet, "teacher" does not define her as a person. Ask any who know her, and they will tell you Regina is passionate about so many things: her son, her grandchildren, truth, children in need, our country's veterans, responsibility, the value of a good education, words, music, dance, the theater, pro football, classic movies, the BBC, track and field, books, books, and more books. Holding multiple degrees, Jeffers often serves as a Language Arts and Media Literacy consultant to school districts and has served on several state and national educational commissions.

Jeffers's writing career began when a former student challenged her to do what she so "righteously" told her class should be accomplished in writing. On a whim, she self-published her first book *Darcy's Passions*. "I never thought anything would happen with it. Then one day, a publishing company contacted me. The rest is history."

Blogs: Every Woman Dreams and Austen Authors
Regina Jeffers's Website
Also Discover Regina on…

Facebook, Pinterest, Twitter, LinkedIn, Goodreads, Bookbub, Instagram, and Amazon Author Central.

Made in the USA
Monee, IL
04 October 2022

15183483R00108